188649

W9-AUA-999

A Conflict of Interests

JEFFREY ASHFORD

A Conflict of Interests

ST. MARTIN'S PRESS   NEW YORK

Library of Congress Cataloging-in-Publication Data

Ashford, Jeffrey.
    A conflict of interests / Jeffrey Ashford.
       p. cm.
    ISBN 0-312-04284-1
    I. Title.
    PR6060.E43C66 1990   89-78027
    823'.914—dc20   CIP

First published in Great Britain by William Collins Sons &
Co. Ltd.

First U.S. Edition
10 9 8 7 6 5 4 3 2 1

A Conflict of Interests

CHAPTER 1

As he looked through the tall window, Bowles mentally razed the low brickbuilt building to the right of his vision, thereby restoring the park to its former state. He then populated it with a herd of red deer, filled in the gaps in the two rows of oaks which bordered the drive, and finally set himself out there, accompanied by Maggie in twin set and tweed skirt, a two-strand rope of pearls about her neck, walking across the grass. The gentleman on his country estate.

The telephone rang to bring him back to reality and a large room with walls panelled in oak with the patina of centuries and a notable mid-eighteenth-century rococo plastered ceiling, but furnished with a battered desk which owed everything to Home Office suppliers and nothing to Chippendale, four chairs of different designs, three battleship-grey metal filing cabinets, a glass-fronted bookcase suffering from endemic woodworm, a carpet with a worn patch in the shape of South America, and two framed prints, one a Burne Jones, the other a Miro, which faced each other with mutual incomprehension.

He crossed to the desk and lifted the receiver of the nearer phone.

Anne, his secretary, said: 'There's a call from Detective Chief Superintendent King. Are you in or out?'

'In.'

'I'll put you through.'

She sounded more cheerful than earlier on, he thought. Perhaps her boyfriend had rung up and they'd managed to resolve their latest misunderstanding. In the past year, they seemed to have quarrelled over everything it was possible for two people who were living together to quarrel over, yet they were still together. He'd long since ceased to wonder at the lives the young led.

'It's Mike here, Pat,' said a deep voice which even over the telephone held a sense of music.

'Hullo, there. How are you?'

'Fine.'

'It's a long time.'

'Just over nine years. I've been in the area on a job, so I thought I'd take the opportunity of calling in and seeing you on the way back, if that's in order?'

'Nothing would be nicer.'

'Good. How about lunch tomorrow?'

'One sec.' Bowles reached over for the desk diary, opened it and read the entries for the next day. 'I'm free until the late afternoon, so that would be fine. Why not eat here? The food's good when the cook's bunions aren't giving her hell and my official entertainment allowance will run to a reasonable bottle of Beaune.'

'Then I'll be with you at twelve-thirty.' King said goodbye and rang off.

Bowles slid off the edge of the desk and went round to the chair behind it, sat. He rested his elbows on the chair, raised his forearms and joined his fingertips together; his elder-statesman attitude, Maggie called it.

He wondered why Mike King should suddenly be bothering to come and see him? They'd known each other for many years and it was true that often people who didn't even really like each other met in order to recall the past in a spirit of nostalgia, but unless King had changed a great deal, he had little time for nostalgia.

Bowles lowered his arms and leaned back in the chair as he stared unseeingly at the worm-eaten bookcase. Maggie had once described Mike King as a man who never bothered to be pleasant unless to do so might gain him something.

They'd first met at training college; he'd been slightly nervous and apprehensive, King had appeared to be completely at ease, even though he must also have known how high was the failure rate. Probably, he'd never suffered the least uncertainty. In theory, there were times when too much self-confidence could be dangerous; if true, he'd not yet met such times . . .

The door opened and Anne came in. She was an almost natural blonde with a figure which despite a love of McDonalds and cream cakes remained fashionably slim. 'Would you mind too much if I left a little early for lunch?' She had a breathless way of speaking, as if she could never utter the words quickly enough. 'I promise I'll get back early.'

'Perhaps just this once, then,' he answered, with mock reluctance.

'You're wonderful!' She flashed him a smile that, had he been younger, might well have made him think of hot sun and hay-lofts. 'Brian's coming home for lunch, but he has to return to work sharp by one because his boss insists on always lunching then. I'd hate to work for someone who lives by the clock like that; I mean, it makes life so boringly certain.'

Did he make her life stimulatingly uncertain, then? He very much doubted it. Presumably, she was hurrying back to a reconciliation. Reconciliation, he'd once read, was the true aphrodisiac of love. He'd settle for a more emotionally level life; forgo the peaks in return for escaping the valleys. He watched her walk over to the door, then remembered something. 'I've arranged a lunch date for tomorrow.'

'Have you made a note of that in the diary?'

'No, I haven't, I'm afraid.'

'How d'you expect me to keep it up to date if you don't tell me what's happening?'

He refrained from pointing out that he had just told her. 'When you come back from lunch, will you get on to the catering manager and tell him I'd like lunch for two in the directors' dining-room. And say I want a bottle of that Beaune.'

'Will do. Now, just before I go, are there any other appointments you need to tell me about?'

'No. But if there are, I'll forget them.'

She gave him a cheeky grin and left. He hoped that reconciliation would prove to be as sweet as she imagined.

Bowles turned off the road and ran the car over the pavement and up the short drive into the garage. Maggie met him in the hall and kissed him on the cheek, not the lips; she was never overtly affectionate. 'What kind of a day have you had?'

'Not a very cheerful one.'

'Oh, dear! What happened?'

'I had to discharge someone.'

'Why.'

'He broke cover and went along to the local pub, got as tight as two ticks, and shouted his head off. According to the landlord, he was telling the world what were his two identities.'

'What will happen to him now?'

'It was his evidence which nailed the mob who carried out that armed bank raid last year where one cashier was killed and another seriously wounded. The others swore they'd get him for grassing—which, of course, is why he came to Hanburrey . . . Outside, on his own, I give him six months at the most.'

'But if the rest of them are in prison, presumably on long sentences, won't he be safe?'

'The police only managed to recover half the stolen money; the remaining half will be enough to buy a dozen contracts on him.'

There were lines of bitterness on his face. She said, almost

angrily: 'Whatever happens, you've no cause to blame yourself. If he's so stupid, it's entirely his own fault.'

'I know. But that doesn't stop me wondering if we might
have got through to him if we'd handled him slightly differ-
ently.'

She sighed. There were times when she regretted that his
sense of duty was so strong. 'Forget work and come on
through and have a drink; supper won't be ready for a
quarter of an hour.'

The sitting-room was a pleasant, informal room, furnished for comfort; Maggie was a woman who valued
warmth of living above style of living. When they had first
moved to Wychley, on his appointment as deputy director
at Hanburrey Manor, it had been she who had chosen
the large Edwardian house in the unfashionable part of the
town rather than a smaller, more modern house on the
fashionable eastern side.

He went over to the cupboard at the far end of the room,
opened the right-hand door, and brought out a bottle of
whisky, two glasses, and a soda siphon; after thirty years of
marriage, there was no need to ask her what she wanted.
He poured out the drinks and crossed to the settee to hand
her a glass. 'Is there anything worth watching?'

'Not before the news.'

Both the *Radio Times* and *TV Times* were handy, but he
didn't bother to check her judgement; their tastes were
similar in most things. He sat.

'John phoned not long before you got back.'

'How is he?'

'The work's going well, the latest girlfriend is great, and
is there any chance we could lend him fifty pounds.'

'Lend?'

'That sounds so much less demanding than give.'

'Why can't he learn to live on what he earns? When we
were young . . .'

'Doesn't have much relation to today. John's generation have a totally different outlook. Money is for spending.'

'Especially when it comes via a piece of plastic.'

'Come on, you're not a hundred and fifty! If they're enjoying life, isn't that what really matters?'

'What matters to me is, at whose expense! I wonder what kind of a girl he's got hold of this time?'

She picked up her knitting. 'His exact description was, an absolute stunner.'

'That's what the last one was until they had that monumental bust-up, after which she became "that infantile bitch". Not that I'd disagree with the description. Damned if I could ever see what attracted him. She was brainless.'

'For heaven's sake, dear man, you surely don't think it was her level of intellect in which he was interested? She was good in bed.'

'How can you possibly know that?'

'The look in her eyes, the way she held herself and moved, the fact that he couldn't stop touching her . . . And if you're about to deliver a lecture on modern decadence, think back to when we were engaged; was it my cooking or the couch in the sitting-room you most looked forward to when my parents were out?'

'You're reminding me about the old joke of the father who listened hard but could hear nothing from the other room so he said to his wife that he ought to go and see what was going on; her reply that he should remember the time when he was young sent him racing.'

She smiled.

'By the way, I heard from an old acquaintance today and he's coming to lunch at the Manor tomorrow. I wondered if you'd like to join us?'

'Who is he?'

'Mike King.'

It took her time to identify the name. 'He's out of the dim and distant past! I'll come along if you really need me, but frankly I'd rather not. It's not that I ever actively disliked him, just . . . Well, I always found we'd practically nothing to say to each other.' She had a round, quietly featured face, notable for the unusual shade of blue of her eyes; often, they more clearly expressed her emotions than she would have wished.

'Fair enough. In any case, I doubt it's a purely social call.' He hesitated, looked at her, then lit a cigarette with guilty speed.

'He's hard. And so very ambitious.'

'Ambition is supposed to be a character plus.'

'Not when it makes a person so selfish that if it'll help him climb a little higher, he doesn't care whom he stands on.'

'You've got him slightly wrong. He won't stand on anyone who's in his way, even if he'll not reach down to help him back on to his feet.'

'I'll stick by my judgement.'

'No, give the man his due; he's smart, sharp, and hard, and he'll cut corners, but in the final event he'll always be professionally honest. Maybe he will always see things from a self-interested angle, but he'll never twist the rules to land a villain.'

'Is that kind of honesty so much more important than having a heart?'

'I've known detectives with hearts who've added or subtracted evidence to make sure a man's found guilty; that means they've betrayed the law they're supposed to be serving.'

'If they're certain he committed the crime, is that so terrible?'

'You know a whole world better than to suggest that guilt can ever rightly be proved by false evidence.'

'Do I? I wonder. Which is the more important—the correct form or the victim?'

'It's a false alternative.'

She was sorry that he admired King. Perhaps his admiration was, subconsciously, masking a degree of jealousy. King had had a meteorically successful career, being the second youngest detective-sergeant, and youngest detective-inspector and detective-superintendent, the county force had known; now, he was second in command of the national anti-terrorist force; he wasn't the only person to believe that one day he would be Commissioner of the Metropolitan force. In contrast, soon after his promotion to detective-sergeant, her husband had finally acknowledged that he would never gain with the police the job-satisfaction he sought—ever the idealist!—and had resigned from the force. Yet although his career in the police had in attainment fallen far short of King's, she 'knew' that he had been the better policeman; he had always believed that pursuing criminals was only part—perhaps even the smaller part—of the job.

He broke the silence. 'I wonder if the visit does have an ulterior motive?'

'You'll learn soon enough.'

He chuckled. 'Mike never was backward in coming forward.'

She stood, empty glass in her right hand. 'I'll go through and see how the meal's coming along. You've time for another drink, if you want one?'

'In modern terminology, that is a stupid question!'

CHAPTER 2

Hanburrey Manor was an E-shaped Elizabethan mansion, built with intricately patterned brickwork and a wealth of

exposed timber. The Dracks-Simpsons had retained owner-
ship of the estate for four hundred years, despite the fact
that even by English aristocratic standards there had in
various generations been an unusually large number of fools
or eccentrics who frequently neglected the house and land.
Then, in the nineteen-fifties, following the deaths of two
owners within ten years of each other, the twenty-four-year-
old Sir Percival, faced with crippling death duties, had been
forced to sell the estate.

It had been bought by a property developer—who disliked history almost as much as he did conservationists
and had seriously underestimated the likely strength of
opposition to his proposed and enlightened plan to demolish
the antiquated and impractical mansion and to replace it
with a large number of modern, exceedingly practical
houses. His application to demolish and build had been
turned down, his appeal from that decision dismissed. Annoyed, and bewildered, he had put the estate back on the
market.

The farmland had been bought almost immediately, but
the park and mansion had remained unsold for eight years,
during which time thieves and vandals had stolen and
smashed almost everything removable or breakable.

Ironically, in view of all the criminal damage suffered, it
had largely been on account of crime that the mansion and
its outbuildings had been saved from terminal decay and
destruction. The Home Office, needing a place where defec-
tors and informers could be given new identities, had bought
the property.

Police informers were feared and hated by criminals; the
police despised them but, recognizing their value—a crime
without a named suspect was seldom solved—did all they
could to encourage them. In small cases, this was not too
difficult, but in bigger ones it was because the informer
might very easily be putting his life at risk. And what

was the use of a nice fat reward (paid by some insurance company) if one was not going to be around to spend it? So in many cases, a man would only inform if he could be guaranteed not only a large reward, but also a future.

The length of a person's stay depended on his or her level of intelligence. The 'students' were taught how to live a new identity and to forget the old; the techniques used owed a lot to the training given to agents who were to be infiltrated into an enemy country. Often, surgery was carried out to remove or modify a physical feature and many a man's or woman's looks had noticeably improved by the time he or she left.

There were few rules governing a person's stay because it was obviously entirely in his or her interests to pass the course with flying colours, but those few were rigorously enforced; if a student divulged his or her old name to anyone except the director, if he or she left the grounds without permission, or if he or she clearly was not cooperating, such person was expelled and from this judgement there was no appeal. In twenty-two years, only nine men and two women had been thrown out; three of them were known to have been subsequently murdered.

Bowles rubbed his eyes which were prickling and thought that Maggie could well be right and he did need glasses for reading, but glasses were the crossing point into middle middle-age and he did not relish the journey. He dropped his hand and stared at the papers on his desk. He was a good administrator (hence his success at his present job) and therefore accepted that paperwork was a necessary part of an ordered life, but there were times when he felt almost overwhelmed. Of course, one of the problems was that many of the papers were for his eyes only. Only he knew both the past and present identities of students; even his deputy director was not, except in the case of his lasting incapacity, allowed to consult the files in the smaller safe. He had been told that not long before one mob leader had offered a hundred thousand pounds for the new name of one man. Every member of staff had been closely vetted, but one didn't have to be a cynic to accept that it was not every honest man who could resist every pressure—not necessarily in the form of money—to betray his honour . . .

The nearer phone rang. 'Detective Chief Superintendent King is here, Mr Bowles,' said Anne.

'Show him in, will you?'

He stood. It was slightly annoying to discover that he felt as if he were about to confront a senior officer and must be seen to show respect. After all, as director of Hanburrey, he occupied a position of considerable prestige and responsibility . . .

Anne came into the room, stood on one side so that King could pass her, took a quick look round the room to make certain all was in order, left, closing the door behind herself.

''Morning, Pat,' said King, in his deep, musical voice.

'Good to see you again.' Bowles came round the desk.

They shook hands. King was shorter and broader than Bowles; his chunky face was fashioned in aggressive lines and his black hair, not yet touched with grey, was brushed back from his forehead and it was clear that it had not yet begun to recede. He was dressed in a good fitting suit of worsted cloth and he could have been a successful business-man, determined to become even more successful. 'I had to pass within ten miles of here, so it seemed an opportunity not to be missed.'

'Glad it wasn't . . . Sit down and then tell me what you'd like to drink?'

'A vodka and tonic, if that's possible?'

Bowles went round the desk to his chair and used the internal phone to ask for a vodka and tonic and a dry sherry. He offered a pack of cigarettes.

'Gave up smoking years ago,' said King. 'Well, how d'you find the job?'

'It's certainly an interesting one.'

'I imagine it's much more up your street.'

Bowles ruefully decided that although that could have been a casual observation, it was more likely to have been an indirect comment on the fact that his capabilities were those of a desk-bound man.

King went on: 'I'll tell you one thing about it. To someone outside, it can stick in the craw to see some miserable grasser getting five-star treatment.'

'Even when the information he's given opens a case right up?'

'Even then.' King smiled briefly. 'I'd forgotten what a reasonable sort of a bloke you were—always able to see the other side of the question. Me—I'm just a simple split who sees things in black or white.'

He was many things, thought Bowles, but a simple man was not one of them.

There was a quick knock on the door and a man entered, tray in his right hand. He passed one glass to King, one to Bowles, then left. King raised his glass. 'To old times . . . Still married to Maggie, I imagine?'

'That's right. And we've one son. What about you?'

'Harriet and I were divorced some time back.'

'I'm sorry to hear that.'

King shrugged his shoulders. 'She'd always been possessive, but thoughts of the menopause made her even more so and she began to moan that I was always with the job and never with her. It ended reasonably amicably and with no kids there weren't any major complications. I remarried three years back. Betty accepts the fact that a policeman's lot is a busy one . . . You look as if you enjoy the life of a lord in this place?'

'Not really. And in the winter it can be cold enough, in

spite of the central heating, to freeze the monkey as well. I guess the Elizabethans must have been a lot tougher than us.'

'The fleas kept them warm . . . Do you live here as well as work?'

'We could have had an apartment, but Maggie's always demanded her own bricks and mortar.'

'Very sensible, with the way property's leapt in value.'

'Her concern's always been with having somewhere to live, whatever happens.'

King put his glass down on the arm of the chair. 'I meant to ring you when I heard you'd been appointed director here. Wanted to send my congratulations to an old colleague, but somehow I never got round to that.'

If Bowles had wanted to congratulate King on one of his promotions, but had failed to do so, he would never have admitted the failure since, by inference, it suggested a large degree of unimportance. He changed the conversation. 'How do you find work in the AT squad after the county force?'

'Twice as hard and four times as frustrating. When a crime's committed, you know you're looking for a villain, but after a terrorist act, just who the hell are you looking for? Last month I nailed the guy who planted a bomb on an Iranian who lived in Battersea. He was a graduate— Oxford and Harvard; rather overdoing the culture—had the manners of a lord, dressed at Gieves, sported a gold Rolex, and read Schopenhauer and Nietzsche in the original. Now who in the hell is going to start looking for a guy like him when a bomb goes off and turns a fat little Iranian queer into a sticky mess?'

'You obviously did.'

'I ended up finding him, which is a very different kettle of fish. And I did that only because he refused to pay what he'd promised. The young man took umbrage and passed on information which gave us the lead we wanted . . . What I found unrealistic about the case was the fact that the only reason I could discover for the murder was that the fat little Iranian was a Shi'ite and the bomber was a Sunni, yet the latter claimed to be irreligious . . . If a man goes into a bank and shoves a gun under one of the staff's nose, anyone can understand his motive.' He drained his glass.

'Will you have the other half?'

'Why not? As Nietzsche ought to have said, the whole is made up of two halves.'

The director's dining-room had originally been the butler's pantry, but its lowly origins were not now evident and from it one had a view over an unspoilt part of the park. The steward—as for some forgotten reason the waiters were called—put the decanter of port by Bowles's side, then withdrew. Bowles passed it.

'This is more like the Ritz than a home for grassers,' said King, as he filled his glass and returned the decanter. 'D'you dine like this every day?'

'Normally, it's lunch in the staff canteen. But I have an entertainment allowance so I can eat here when the occasion warrants it.'

'And by your excellent reckoning, an old friendship does!'

Bowles was perplexed. King was now speaking like a man who'd drunk a shade too much, yet in the old days he could consume three-quarters of a bottle of Scotch without even beginning to slur his words. Could he be uncertain or nervous? It was difficult to think of his suffering from either weakness.

'Shall I tell you something?' King raised his glass and drank before he spoke again. 'You're one of the few people I know with the intelligence to appreciate the fact that law and justice aren't the same thing.'

'I'd have thought most people realized that.'

'Then you'd have thought wrongly. The average man reckons law is justice. But although one can lead a civilized life without law, one cannot without justice.'

'Can you have justice without law?'

King waved that aside as an irrelevance. 'So justice is the more important. The one buttress that any society must enjoy if it's to be civilized and free is justice. You'd agree, of course?'

'In general terms.'

'Sometimes law conflicts with justice because, of necessity, its rules and regulations create a rigid framework and that ensures that there are anomalies. Right?'

'Since no law can be perfect, yes. But then, can justice always be perfect?'

'By definition, it has to be. If it seems not to be, then the law serving it has to be wrong. In which case, the law has to be altered or by-passed.'

Bowles finally understood what had brought King to Hanburrey Manor and he knew both irritation and amusement; irritation that the other should believe him capable of ever betraying his trust, amusement that the lead-up should be so long-winded and hypocritical. He passed the decanter, then took it back and refilled his own glass.

King leaned back in his chair. He had a relatively small mouth, slightly out of proportion with the size of his head, and his lips were thin; if angry or earnest, his lips tightened until he looked cruel as well as aggressive. 'Does the name ALFA mean anything to you?'

Bowles thought for a moment. 'I don't think so.'

'Animal Liberation For All. The group originally campaigned on an anti-vivisection ticket; as such, it gained very little publicity and so it decided to spread its wings and include all rights of all animals; make hunting and shooting illegal, prohibit the importation of the skins of any animals, stop all intensive farming, and so on. They waved banners at meets, walked across grouse beats, picketed factory farm units. But because competition in that field of protest is fierce, they still didn't get the publicity they wanted; in consequence, there was formed one—soon, there were more—direct action cell. Members of this went into a pig farm one night and released all the pigs; I'm told that the mess which had to be cleared up made the Augean Stables child's play. There was the usual letter to the local press claiming responsibility and this gained them a small paragraph in one of the inside pages. They released all the mink on a mink farm; over the next few months the escaped mink killed much of the wildlife in the area—no comment from ALFA over that! Then they broke into a laboratory engaged on research which used animals and planted a fire-bomb which only went off at half-cock, but still destroyed a lot of records and years of work. This time they got plenty of publicity and the local police plenty of stick.

'You'll know there's often a consequential connection between a blinkered group which is highly committed and terrorism. In its efforts to gain its objectives, the group discovers that success depends on publicity, publicity on news, and newscasters welcome events that frighten, disgust, or provoke almost any emotion other than complacency.

'We were called in at this stage because it looked as if here was a group which could easily become very dangerous. I had a headshrinker draw up a profile on the kind of person likely to progress from animal rights campaigner to terrorist. He said that people who identify themselves so deeply with the welfare of animals are often compensating for their inability to get on with their fellow humans. When their efforts to gain publicity meet with some success, they feel gratification and the stirrings of a sense of importance; they begin to think themselves superior rather than inferior. If this sense of importance grows unchecked, they may reach the point where they believe they are no longer bound by manmade laws and are justified in taking any steps to reach their goals. Necessary acts of violence are one of the weapons of superman, to quote that old bore, Nietzsche.

'Knowing what kind of person one may be looking for isn't much help until and unless one has some sort of specific lead; for a time we didn't have any, not least because ALFA claims thousands of members countrywide. Then we struck lucky and homed in on a man called Sanderson who, rather ironically, didn't begin to fit the picture the psychiatrist had painted; a perfectly straightforward type. He admitted he was a member of ALFA because he was against cruelty to animals; what decent person wasn't? He strongly deprecated hunting, shooting, and probably fishing, factory farming, and all experiments on animals which weren't absolutely necessary for medical reasons. But he'd no knowledge of any action group within ALFA and would never carry out an illegal act in furtherance of animal welfare; all advances in the country's treatment of animals had to be gained within the existing legal framework . . . We weren't getting anywhere, so we searched his place.'

'Without a warrant, at a guess?'

King looked annoyed, then he relaxed and even smiled briefly. 'As Confucius say, if man catch fish, bait OK . . . We found evidence of his association with a hard group and this included the names of two other members. We questioned those two and persuaded them to talk very much more freely than he had.'

'How?'

'What answer are you expecting—thumbscrews? They weren't too voluble to begin with, so I told 'em Sanderson had volunteered their names. There's nothing sets a person talking so eagerly as when he believes he's been betrayed.'

Bowles lit a cigarette. How far could a lie be justified in uncovering a truth? It was a question for a philosopher, not an ex-policeman. He passed the decanter of port. 'How much were they able to tell you?'

'Not a tenth of what I'd hoped, although they did identify all the other members of their cell and admitted to some minor jobs and one major one—the fire-bomb. Security was really tight; there was no lateral connection between hard cells and information was on a need-to-know basis. They'd no idea who was in charge of the hard campaign, beyond the fact that it was no one on the national committee of ALFA—probably true since that's filled with well-known people who wouldn't take such a risk. Hours of questioning produced only one other useful piece of information: Sanderson was very friendly with a woman who, they believed, was close to those at the top.

'We went back and questioned him again. He admitted knowing several women members of ALFA, but swore that none of them had any connection with direct action. Since he was a normal sort of a bloke, I tried to show him that it was in everyone's interests, including the people directly concerned, that we identify potential terrorists before they graduate into becoming actual terrorists. He wouldn't listen.

'There was a trial and in view of the fire-bomb the accused were given prison sentences; that is, with the exception of Sanderson because we acknowledged his assistance and he could not have taken part in the fire-bomb raid. He collected a suspended sentence only. That night, he received an anonymous telephone call. The price of betrayal was death.

'He was offered the chance of coming here and gaining a new identity. After all, he had helped us, even if inadvertently.'

'Ah!' said Bowles, as if this was a possibility that had not occurred to him.

'For a while, nothing more was heard of the hard side of ALFA and people hoped that the imprisonment of four of the members had shocked everyone else into common sense.

Then a laboratory was broken into and, after all the animals were released, burned to the ground. There was a night watchman, but he was too old to put up any real resistance and they tied him up and gagged him and left him in an outbuilding; no rough stuff. They'd worn ski-masks, so he hadn't a clue what any of them looked like, but he had noticed that one of the two men who'd tied him up had had an unusual tattoo on the inside of his wrist. The old boy might be a bit shaky on his pins, but he's all there upstairs and he was able to describe the tattoo so exactly that we were able to identify its owner from Records; a greengrocer who, four years before and when a member of another organization, had been in trouble. I decided not to pick him up, but to send one of my lads to infiltrate the hard cell.'

'Has he been successful?'

'Only up to a point. He's accepted as a committed member of ALFA, but hasn't yet been able to get into the hard cell itself. As he puts it, he's still on probation.'

'Then he's every chance of making it sooner or later?'

'Later will be too late. I've a feeling about this bunch. They're potentially bloody dangerous.'

'You're suggesting they're becoming as attracted to the use of violence as to the attainment of their stated objectives?'

'In one. Violence is as addictive as a drug . . . I saw a fair bit of Sanderson and as I said before, I judged him to be talking straight and while he'd work as hard as he could for animals, he was able to see that the use of violence destroyed any basis of justification. I'm sure that if I could talk to him now, tell him about the latest raid, explain the probable escalation of force, he'd realize that if he knows who's running the hard cells, he should name names.'

'I wonder?'

'This lot's going to become more and more violent and innocent people are going to be killed.'

'That's still supposition.'

'The pattern's there if you've eyes to see it and it can lead only in one direction ... To save innocent lives, I must identify the people in charge. Sanderson can give names. So when and how can I get in contact with him?'

'You know I can't give such information. My terms of reference are explicit.'

'Maybe you didn't hear. Lives are at stake.'

'Only if you're absolutely right. Yet you admit you're basing everything on little more than a hunch.'

'On thirty years' experience ... Look, if you're that worried about anyone finding out you've told me, forget it. No one beyond these four walls will ever know.'

'I don't work that way.'

King's expression said it all. In his opinion, that was the reason why Bowles had resigned when only a detective-sergeant.

CHAPTER 3

Betty King looked across the dining table and said, in her husky voice: 'Don't let anyone fool you into thinking that you're the life and soul of the party.'

King replied bad-temperedly: 'So what d'you want me to do? Put on a false nose and dance the hornpipe?'

'It would be more entertaining, though not necessarily from an artistic point of view. Have some more wine and see if that lightens your horizons.'

'I don't want any more.'

'Then it's the martyr complex tonight?'

King's anger finally surfaced. 'God Almighty, we're supposed to be nearing the end of the twentieth century, not beginning the nineteenth! Father dear, I cannot lie, I did cut down the tree with my penknife.'

'Surely there's a slight mix-up over dates? Or was it a date tree? . . . Not appreciated? Never mind. But if you're going to deny yourself out of pique, I am not. Will you pass the bottle?'

He did so.

She refilled her glass. 'What do you think of this wine? It's Australian.'

'So long live Strineland.'

'I want to go there next year to see Ayers Rock, hear a concert in the Sydney Opera House, and cuddle a Koala bear.'

'They're unsafe to handle.'

'Trust you to concentrate on the depressing details! Introduce you into a harem and you'd ponder the possible incidence of pox.'

'You're talking ridiculously.'

'It takes two to tango.'

She mocked him when he was in one of his down-moods, whereas Harriet had always tried to humour him and had concealed any sense of resentment she might have felt. But one had only to look at Betty to realize that she had a combative nature. Very smart, in a sharp, glossy manner; jet black hair drawn tight around her head; make-up flattering but far from subtle; costume jewellery deliberately too large; clothes tight and designed to promote a body still shapely although she was nearer forty than she willingly admitted.

'Change your mind?' she suggested, as she passed the bottle back. 'I don't want any more and it's surely not worth leaving a little to go sour just to prove what a man of inflexible principles you are?'

She had an irritating knack of making him feel that

further bad temper would just make him look ridiculous. He emptied the bottle into his glass.

'By the way, Felicity rang earlier. She's asked us to lunch on Sunday. Will you be free?'

'I can't say yet.'

'It's not vital. She hopes you will be along, but it won't ruin her arrangements if you're held up at the last moment. She's also inviting the Harpleys.'

He said, surprised: 'She's asked George? He's a bit of a villain.'

'Of course, that's his attraction. Janet says that in spite of a ricked back in the summer, he had two torrid affairs.'

'I meant, in business.'

'I'm interested in his love-life. There's always something challenging about a dedicated philanderer.'

'Just make certain you don't think of accepting the challenge.'

'How would you react if I did?' She studied him. 'I think you could become rather fearsome and I'd have to run to Mummy for protection.'

He had to smile at the absurd thought.

'That's better! The first peep of the sun through the thinning clouds . . . What's got you so uptight at work?'

Harriet had never asked him about his work because the only way in which she'd ever known to fight a rival had been to ignore it. 'I had to see a man to try to persuade him to use some common sense.'

'And obviously you didn't succeed.'

'Too much the man of honour.'

'How very boring.'

His voice rose. 'How can anyone be such a sanctimonious fool?'

'Easily . . . What exactly has been happening?'

He briefly told her.

'Surely this Sanderson man would see that if the idiots

are working up to something really nasty, a hell of a lot of people can be killed or very seriously hurt?'

'Bowles's principles are engraven on tablets of stone. He's entrusted with a duty and so nothing, absolutely bloody nothing, will make him betray that duty.'

'Sounds like a survivor from the dinosaur age. Was he like that when he was a policeman?'

'Exactly like, which is why he wasn't ever a good one.'

'You're becoming ever more cynical.'

'More a realist. A good split has to learn to walk through muck and clean his shoes afterwards.'

'You can talk like that, but there are things you wouldn't do, not if your life depended on it. You'd never betray yourself as a policeman.' She spoke with sudden—and to those who didn't really know her, unexpected—pride.

They finished the wine, cleared the table and carried dishes, plates, and cutlery through to the kitchen, where she stacked the dishwasher. Then they went through to the sitting-room.

He sat, used the remote control to switch on the television. Almost as the picture appeared, the telephone rang. Seeing him about to stand, she said, 'I'll get it. You're so tired.'

'It's all right. It's almost certainly for me.'

'Why won't they ever leave you alone?'

'I asked one of the lads to call me at this time.' He left the room, crossed the hall, and picked up the receiver. 'Yeah?'

'It's Reg, Guv.'

'What's the news?'

'There isn't any. And before you comment on my ancestors, I'm dealing with a bunch of clams who've been eating super-glue.'

'Can't you pick up even a whisper?'

'Not even the whisper of a whisper . . . You said you were

hoping to get some information that would be useful—have you?'

'No.'

'Then that makes two of us who are running hard but standing still!'

'Keep digging, Reg, but keep you head down.'

'Are you kidding? It's lower than a snake's belly . . . I'll ring again in two days.'

'Make it a couple of hours earlier.' King said goodbye, replaced the receiver. It was over a month since Newton had made contact with the known member of the hard cell, but so far he'd not managed to make much further progress . . . He returned to the sitting-room.

'That was the chap I was telling you about just now who's trying to infiltrate the hard cell.'

'Any luck?'

'No.' He clenched his right fist and slammed it down on the arm of the chair. 'All I was asking that bloody Pat to do was to whisper the name and address. No one would ever have learned.'

'But he'd have known he had.'

'Honourable men! They cause more trouble in the world than all the villains put together.'

CHAPTER 4

Steven Collins turned off the road and drove into the garage which was a World War II army hut, beginning to look as if it dated back to World War I. He picked up the wrapped box of chocolates from the front passenger seat, climbed out of the Escort, left the garage, and walked along the gravel path, past the small orchard, to the garden which encircled the cottage.

Judith, an apron over her frock, met him in the small hall. She kissed him with warmth. 'You're late and I was beginning to wonder if the old girl had dropped a valve, or whatever it is that cars do when they're geriatric.'

'I was about to leave the office when boss-man turned up with some figures he wanted checking last week. He's in a muck sweat because he's afraid he's lost money on a deal.'

'And has he?'

'That I could live to see the day! All that's happened is, he's not made quite as much as usual. But I expect that even that knowledge has given him palpitations.'

'It must be awful to value money above everything else.'

'Save your pity; he's no idea that there are alternatives. And talking about the rich, a present.' He held out the box.

'How wonderful! For why?'

'Because it's Thursday.'

'I adore inconsequential presents.' She undid the satiny binding and unwrapped the patterned paper. 'Chocolate from Luigi! Not those heavenly rum truffles?'

'In one.'

'But how could you be so extravagant?'

'Because I'm a poor man.'

'What are they going to do to all my lose-weight resolutions?'

'Hopefully, scuttle them. You haven't half a pound spare, let alone half a stone; the blubber's all in your mind.'

She kissed him. 'That's for the truffles.' She kissed him again. 'And that's for lying about my weight so convincingly that I can believe you until the next time I get on the scales.'

The sitting-room door—original, made from oak, pitted —opened and Bob looked out. 'Where's my supper, Mum?'

'I'm just about to get it . . . Say hullo to Steve.'

Bob looked quickly at Collins, his blue eyes, almost the same shade as his mother's, hostile.

'Say hullo.' Her voice had sharpened.

He mumbled something that could just about be accepted as a welcome, stepped back and began to close the door.

'What d'you want for supper? There's fish fingers, baked beans on toast, or grilled sardines on toast.'

'I don't mind.' He shut the door.

She looked at her husband. 'I'm sorry,' she said wearily.

'Forget it.'

'That's easier said than done, isn't it? Why does he have to be so cruel?'

'Because he's young.'

'Thank God you're understanding.'

He wondered briefly if he warranted such praise. There were times when he suffered an almost overwhelming urge to take Bob by the scruff of the neck and shake some common sense into him; what stopped him was not his sympathetic understanding of Bob's emotional problems, but the certainty that to act thus would cause her great distress. Bob, the only child of her first marriage, had been two when his father had died, four and a half when she'd married again. Being sensible people, they'd expected him to react unfavourably to the appearance of a stepfather. To their delighted relief, there had to begin with been no tantrums, no resentment, and no withdrawal. They'd congratulated themselves not only on their luck but also on their handling of a difficult situation which so many others found insoluble —only to discover that their self-congratulations had been premature. On his sixth birthday—perhaps excitement had been the trigger—he had screamed at his stepfather and it had suddenly become clear that resentment had been only temporarily damned, not escaped.

She sighed. 'Who said that if it weren't for people, life would be easy?'

'You have an attack of the glooms for which I prescribe a drink.'

She reached out with her free hand and touched his arm. 'I was lucky when I met you.'

'Exceptionally so.'

'My God, the man doesn't exactly dislike himself! . . . Come into the kitchen while I check how the meal's going. We're having kidneys and salami—you like that, don't you?'

'Especially if you've added several teeth of garlic.'

'Only one. You don't want to breathe garlic fumes over boss-man.'

'Cooking kills the odour. In any case, if he recoils I'll tell him the latest medical evidence proves garlic is the best possible preventive against cholesterol. Being the original hypochondriac, that'll get him eating garlic until he stinks like the Paris metro.'

In the kitchen, she brought out a glass casserole from the oven. She removed the lid, tasted the stew, used mills to add salt and pepper, tasted again. 'That's better.'

'You're a wonderful cook, which is why I married you.'

'There are worse reasons. When I'm old and wrinkled, but still able to cook a coq au vin, I'll have the security of knowing that you'll think twice before running after sexy eighteen-year-olds.'

'I'll think twenty times.'

'Exaggeration is the handmaiden of a lie . . . Instead of talking nonsense, suppose you go and get those drinks you promised. I'd like a sherry, please.'

He went through to the dining-room and across to the court cupboard, with beautifully carved strap work, which was one of the pieces of furniture from her first home. The drinks were kept in the right-hand side, the glasses in the left-hand; he filled two schooners.

Back in the kitchen, he handed her a glass. She raised it. 'Cheers . . . Steve, be an angel, will you, and fix up Bob's supper while I cope with ours?' I'm sorry I'm so far behind, but I was getting worried and keeping one eye on the road and I kept hearing cars which I thought were the Old Girl, only none of them was . . .'

She didn't have to finish for him to understand. He'd been late and she'd begun to fear that something had happened to him on the journey home. Routine had gone by the board. Under her calm manner there was a depth of emotion which meant that there were times when she worried extravagantly . . . 'Bob didn't say what he wanted to eat, so what shall I get him?'

'He's had rather a lot of fried things recently, so perhaps it had better be beans on toast. I think there's a tin left in the store cupboard.'

The store cupboard was also the china cupboard—in the cottage, space was at a premium. He found a tin of beans on the middle shelf and brought this out.

'Good,' she said, as she topped and tailed French beans. 'Put them into a saucepan and warm them and make a couple of slices of toast.'

Seven minutes later, the toast was buttered and the beans were warm. He emptied the beans from the saucepan on to the toast. There was nothing which so quickly evoked the past as a smell. Despite all the training he'd received at Hanburrey Manor, designed to replace the true past with a false one, his mind slipped back to a dark, drizzly night and a small, somewhat dingy café. The window had needed cleaning, the sauce bottle had clotted sauce about its cap, the salt shaker's holes had become bunged up, and the paper tablecloth looked as if it hadn't been changed that week; but the baked beans and sausages had tasted delicious. Moira, without a known drop of Irish blood in her, had looked even more Irish than usual, with her midnight hair, deep, deep blue eyes, and finely drawn face, vulnerable because her passions were so quick and extreme. She hadn't understood what he'd been saying, which had hardly been surprising since he couldn't logically explain, or even sort out, his own feelings . . .

'Are you waiting for me to take it through?' she asked.

His mind jerked back to the present. He put the plate on a tray, collected a knife and fork from the dining-room, carried the tray through to the sitting-room. 'Grub's up.'

Bob neither acknowledged his arrival, nor his words; he continued to stare at the television.

'If you can't hear me, I'll have to switch off the telly so that you can.'

Sullenly, he accepted the tray.

'I wouldn't object to a word of thanks.'

Bob mumbled something.

Collins returned to the kitchen, picked up his glass, and drank. There were times when he doubted the essential belief that children were a gift from heaven.

He ate the last mouthful and said: 'That was truly delicious.'

Judith smiled contentedly. 'Keep saying nice things and I'll risk trying to make you a *Filet de bœuf flambé à L'Avignonnaise.*'

'You're on.'

'What would you like now? There's strawberry ice-cream and/or cheese?'

'Just cheese for me; which for you?'

'Neither and then I can allow myself one rum truffle.'

'Two taste better.'

'Get thee behind me, Satan; way out of sight and hearing.'

He went through to the kitchen and returned with the cheeseboard and a tin of biscuits. As he sat, she said: 'I had coffee with Madge this morning and she and Roy are going to house-sit for friends who are off to the States for a month. Madge suggested we went and spent a weekend with them. Apparently it's a beautiful, listed Georgian house, the garden's quite famous, and there are even a couple to do the cooking and cleaning. Madge says it's the kind of place one reads about in the glossy magazines.'

'It sounds tremendous.'

'Would boss-man give you a Friday afternoon off so that we could drive up and arrive before it becomes too late?'

'If I kowtow abjectly, I might be able to dent his steely heart. How far away is it?'

'In Shropshire, but unless there's a lot of motorway under repair, it's a quick journey.'

'Which part of the county?'

She was surprised by the sudden change in his tone. 'Wem's apparently the nearest place of any size. I'll tell her, then, that we'd love to have an up-market weekend.'

He cut a slice of Cheddar. 'Just hang on before you say anything definite.'

'Why?'

'I'll have to see how the work looks,' he answered vaguely as he reached for the biscuits.

Upstairs in Brecks Cottage there were three south-facing bedrooms and a bathroom; they slept in the east, Bob in the middle one. They were both in bed and he had opened a paperback and begun to read when she said: 'Is there something odd about Shropshire?'

'How d'you mean?'

'It's the second time.'

He looked up. 'Quite possibly. But the second time for what?'

She fingered the hem of the sheet. 'Do you remember when we went up to the Lake District last summer?'

'I know you think I have a bad memory, but I'm hardly likely to have forgotten that as yet.'

'On the run back, I wanted to stop and see an old schoolfriend and you said we couldn't, we were running out of time. We weren't really. And you didn't raise any objection until I mentioned that she lived in Hodnet. That's not very far from Wem. Earlier this evening, you were all for a weekend with Madge and Roy until you heard they'd be near Wem, then you backed right off.'

'All I said was, I'd have to see how the work looked.'

'Is there something about that part of the county of which you are . . . well, afraid?'

'That's a hell of a funny thing to say.'

'I know it sounds a bit daft, but . . . Steve, why is it you try never to talk about the past? You never bring up personal memories of before we met.'

'That's because I led a very boring and humdrum life. Mr dull average man, that's me.'

'You're not dull and you're not average.'

'Thank you, madam, for those kind words.'

His tone had made it obvious that he was not going to answer her question. Perhaps, she thought, the countryside around Wem had played a significant and sad part in his early life and he preferred not to return since to do so might recall such period in too sharp a focus . . .

CHAPTER 5

Reginald Newton finished his routine and very brief call to King and then inserted fifty p and dialled his fiancée. After six rings, the call was answered. 'Sandra, it's me.'

'Darling, I've been waiting and waiting.'

'Sorry about that, but life's been rather hectic. How are things?'

'Fine.'

'Feeling lonely?'

'Desperately.'

'Come on up here and have a cuddle. The landlady's broad-minded.'

'If that's all you really want to see me for, I'll stay here.'

He remembered their last evening together. It had been he who called a halt, not she. His mates would have jeered at him had they known, but he wanted their final act of love to take place only after they were married . . .

'Reg, are you still there?'

'I was just thinking of our last night together.'

She giggled. 'Love, I had another word with Mr Barnet; he says it's almost certain that the cottage will be becoming empty.'

'Fine. But is he going to let it to us?'

'If the solicitor agrees it's all right for him to do that, yes.'

'Did you tell him that we promise to quit after being given six months' notice.'

'Yes, but he still has to make certain how the law stands now. He was really nice about it. He said that he knew we really mean what we say now, but if by the time he wants possession we have a baby and nowhere to move to, and the council can't or won't help, it would only be human nature for us to try and stay if the law gives us that right.'

'I suppose he's got something there. I bloody well wouldn't stand by and watch anyone shoving you out into the cold . . . I'll keep my fingers crossed that the solicitor says it's OK.'

'Me, too. Darling, when are you coming back?'

'When the job's finished.'

'Yes, I know. But when will that be?'

'I don't expect it'll be too long now.'

'You've been away for months and months.'

'It feels more like years and years.'

'Why can't somebody take over from you?'

'It's not that kind of a job.'

Time ran out and he had to insert another coin.

'Don't be long coming back.'

'I won't; solemn promise.'

'Mum says she wants it to be a white wedding.'

'But that's what you'd really prefer, isn't it? I mean, a registry office wedding isn't much different from buying the groceries.'

'If you think that all you're going to get is a sack of old potatoes . . . You realize a proper reception means Uncle Alf will want to propose the toast?'

'Fill him full enough of booze and he won't be able to talk too dirty.'

'You don't know him. He told a joke last night that made even Mum blush.'

'Let's hear it.'

'Not likely. You're not old enough.'

'I'm six months older than you.'

'Only in years, not in maturity.'

'You reckon?'

'All right, who was it had to decide that we couldn't live in thin air and really had to find a house or flat before fixing a date for the wedding? Who had to decide that we'd better stop celebrating our engagement three times a week and start saving? Who had to—'

'I surrender, unconditionally. It was you, every time. You're the brains, I'm just the brawn . . . Look, I'm going to have to ring off soon because I haven't any more coins for the flaming box.'

'Love me?'

'So much I want to jump over the moon.'

'Then you haven't got a redhead up where you are?'

'I haven't looked at another woman since I left you.'

'Tell me something I can believe.'

'If half a dozen blondes, all starkers, walked past me now, I wouldn't give them a second look.'

'Because you'd never stop gawping in the first case.'

He chuckled. 'I'd better close down. I'll ring again the day after tomorrow, same time.' His affectionate goodbye was cut short and he cursed the soulless BT as he replaced the receiver. He pulled the collar of his mackintosh as high up his neck as it would go to counter the damp wind, left the call-box and walked past the line of shops to the crossroads.

CHAPTER 6

Lees stopped to watch Newton turn the corner and go out of sight. A man knocked into him. 'Look where you're bleeding going, mate.'

He stepped aside to let the other pass. That was, he thought, the third time in the past two weeks that on his way back from work he'd seen Newton make a call from one of the two kiosks. Yet he knew for fact that there was a telephone in the house in which Newton lodged and he was allowed to use it, so why not phone from there?

Lees crossed the road—ever since a TV programme on the incidence of heart attacks in the over 40s, he'd walked to and from work unless it was raining—and took the path which cut caterwise across the green. In the old days, the inhabitants of Radlington had been divided between those who lived north of the green and those who lived south. It had been a social distinction; to the north were professional people in detached houses with gardens, to the south manual workers, mostly in terrace houses. However, recently, which was to say over the past thirty years, the distinction had become distorted because of development and the introduction of light industry and now it was even in danger of becoming reversed; many of the houses to the north were looking shabby and on the outskirts to the south a number of large 'executive' houses for senior management types had been built. For the older inhabitants from the north, however, the occupants of these new houses were parvenus.

Once north of the green, he turned into Brampton Lane. Years ago, the Padlows had briefly lived in the fourth house on the right. He'd become friendly with Tim, but then his mother had said it would be better if he didn't see any more of him. It was only long afterwards that he'd understood why. Tim's father had been a butcher who'd started a chain of shops and made a great deal of money, leading him to the besetting sin of all *nouveaux riches*—the naïve belief that money could raise a person's social position. A person in trade could not be a gentleman, however rich.

At the end of Brampton Lane was a T-junction and here he turned right. Lucy had lived in the very large Edwardian house. He'd wanted her to come to one of his birthday parties, but his mother had said that that wasn't a very good idea. Rumour had had it that Lucy's mother was not really married to her father. He remembered—with a stab of shame—that that particular party had ended with his hiding in a clothes cupboard to escape from the other three boys who'd discovered that much more fun than pass the parcel or hunt the thimble was thumping Jeremy until he blubbered . . .

He reached Three Firs, opened the squealing wrought-iron gate, walked up the flagstone path to the three steps and the porch. He unlocked the front door with the key which his mother had presented to him, with considerable emotion, on his twenty-first birthday. She'd suggested, in a spirit of self-sacrifice, that that evening he forgot her and took out Sylvia to a dinner-dance at the Grand in Shrewsbury. Sylvia had been vivacious and slightly giddy (a favourite word of his mother's). Half-way through the evening, she'd pleaded a headache and asked to be taken home. A few days later he'd learned from someone else that her complaint had been boredom, not a headache . . .

'Is that you, dear?'

He went into the drawing-room. His mother looked frail, yet she was as tough as old boots and a few weeks ago the doctor had said that she'd live to make a hundred plus. He dreaded the future—the endless need to cater to all her whims and needs or the emptiness that her death would provoke.

'Have you had a good day?' she asked.

He sat and was about to describe his day—a repetition of every other day at the office—when she started to describe the awful day she had had. He poured out two sweet sherries and they drank. He said he'd go and prepare the meal and she said she wasn't hungry—it was only women who were ever hungry; ladies were never so coarse—and would he switch on the television because it was almost time for one of her favourite programmes. He used the remote control —on the table by her side—to switch on the set.

In the kitchen, he opened the refrigerator and brought out a dish in which two pork chops had been marinading in spiced red wine. He put the chops on a grille to drain, checked in a cookery book how to make the sauce. He scraped half a dozen new potatoes and shelled some peas, put the potatoes on to boil.

He laid two trays. Naturally, originally they'd always eaten their meals in the dining-room, but then he'd persuaded her to accept a television set in the house and within a month even her belief in standards had not been strong enough to overcome her reluctance to miss a programme.

He poured the peas into the second saucepan, added salt, lit the grill. He began to mix the sauce, set the meat under the grill, returned to the sauce. As he worked, he wondered again why Newton was apparently regularly making phone-calls from a public call-box when there was a telephone in the house in which he was living? He couldn't think of Newton without becoming very bitter. After all, it was Reg who'd set out to be friendly; it was Reg who'd suggested coffee, spending a couple of hours in a pub, or going for a walk in the countryside. At first suspicious—normally, no one wanted to be friends with him; was the motive sexual?—he'd then accepted the friendship with intense gratitude. But just as he'd begun to discover some of the things he'd been missing in life, he'd learned that he'd been betrayed. Reg was becoming friendly with some of the others . . .

On first joining ALFA, he'd been warned against spies; the sadistic bastards who enjoyed inflicting pain on defenceless animals would go to any underhand lengths to defeat their opponents. The warning had been repeated at greater length and with much more emphasis when he'd been accepted into the hard cell. Could Reg, who had shown himself to be a very inquisitive man, in truth be a spy?

CHAPTER 7

Collins turned over a forkful of earth, broke it up with the tines, straightened up and used the back of his hand to wipe the sweat from his forehead. If ever they moved, the first thing about any new property to check would be the soil in the garden—if it proved to be Kentish clay, the purchase would be vetoed even if the house was a period masterpiece.

'It's nearly seven,' Judith called out from the house.

He needed no further encouragement to stop work. He carried the fork over to the garden shed, changed his shoes, crossed the concrete path to the kitchen.

'I didn't know whether you wanted to watch the programme on sailing ships which comes on in a few minutes,' she said, as she looked up from the ironing she was doing.

'Very much so. Thanks for remembering.'

'There was a preview this morning and they showed a short clip of a full rigged ship rounding the Horn. It looked like absolute hell. Do you really think you'd have wanted to go to sea in sail?'

'It was my one overriding ambition when I was young. But since it was impossible to fulfil it, I viewed with total equanimity the prospect of being soaked to the skin, frozen to the marrow, and sharing my biscuits with the weevils.'

'You're saying you were ready to face hardships only because you could be certain you'd never have to? . . . Steve, why do you so often denigrate yourself?'

'Do I?'

'Yes, you do and it's so stupid! If you could have sailed on a windjammer, you would have done, as much as anything because of the hardships involved.'

'You're now suggesting I am of a perverse nature.'

'That's only the half!' She put the iron down on the insulated pad at the end of the board. 'Do yourself justice, Steve; you're a fighter.' She noticed his quick expression. 'Why look like that when I say you're a fighter?'

'Nothing to do with your words, all to do with the twinge in my back. Digging unveils a whole family of new muscles.'

'Would you like me to rub some embrocation into your back?'

'It's not that bad, thanks.'

'The suffering in silence syndrome?'

He smiled. 'Provided people realize how brave I'm being.' He walked over to the inside door. 'I'm going up for a quick wash.'

As he waited in the bathroom for the basin to fill with hot water, he looked at his reflection in the mirror. A fighter? Hardly. He hadn't fought very long to prove that he was not the traitor others believed him. Instead, he'd accepted the police's advice to go to Hanburrey and gain a new identity because if he didn't, he would be in very great danger of being murdered. When did common sense become cowardice? How far had he been influenced in his decision by the bitterly muddled memories of his affair with Moira?

It was strange how it had all started; many of life's shifting points did start casually. A fine but cold Saturday morning in January, the previous day's snow still on the ground. An enthusiastic walker, he'd left home—by then both his parents had died—and had set out on a six-mile circuit which took him through a large estate. A cocks-only shoot had been in progress and as he'd approached one of the woods he'd heard the tapping of the beaters' sticks, the claps of sounds as frightened pheasants finally and frantically broke cover and took to the air, and the explosive sounds of shooting. The road had turned to bring him in sight of the guns and he had seen birds dropping. Initially, the scene had not provoked within him any definite emotion. He didn't shoot, but he hadn't ever thought to condemn it; it was a traditional country sport and he was a countryman. But if he hadn't condemned, neither had he ever considered what was really involved in the 'sport'.

When well past that wood—perhaps a quarter of a mile along the road—he'd seen a pheasant sitting in the snow, ten yards into a field. A Chinese ringneck cock, it had been decked in such a wild extravagance of colour that not even the most brilliant of artists could have accurately reproduced them. With virgin snow as a background, it became a picture of breathtaking beauty . . . And then he had noticed that the snow before its breast was stained red and had realized what held the bird motionless. He'd continued to watch, experiencing as he did so a growing anger. The head had slowly leaned forward, the eyes had dimmed, and the beautiful bird had died in agony in the name of 'sport'.

During the following days he had sought out and read pamphlets put out by anti-vivisection and anti-blood sports groups. Common sense and his knowledge as a countryman told him that much of what was written needed to be treated with caution or even discounted, but even so there was enough left to horrify any man who considered himself civilized and humane. Calves deliberately reared to be anæmic because veal eaters demanded white meat; rabbits clamped immobile with their eyelids forced back so that substances could be introduced on to their eyes to find out how irritating those substances were; dogs with painful congenital defects used to breed those defects into their progeny . . .

Chance had introduced him to ALFA rather than to any other organization actively interested in animal rights. He liked their common-sense approach to a subject which was all too often scrambled by emotions. It was their declared aim to have made illegal the exploitation of, and the infliction of pain on, any animal; saving such experiments as were certified as being of necessary importance to the advancement of medical science.

A few weeks after joining ALFA, he'd met Moira, the colleen without a drop of Irish blood. The intensely blue eyes had excited him, the warm mouth had welcomed him, the sculptured body had enraptured him . . . What is the difference between a man who is insane and a man who is in love? Who's insane enough to say there is a difference? Life had glowed in psychedelic colours; glowed so brightly that passion had exploded him into scenes he had hardly ever imagined, let alone experienced. And then one day it seemed as if he had suddenly and inexplicably been granted a sufficient return of sanity to understand that she had led him to the rim of a crater and was now persuading him to jump into it with her; he sensed that there was a streak of madness in her, fuelled not by any normal passion, but by the desire to degrade herself and through herself, him . . .

While in her thrall, he'd joined a small inner cell of ALFA members whose declared aim had been to pursue their cause more vigorously. When he'd learned that to some this had meant not merely intensifying the kind of action they were already taking, but moving on to acts of violence, he'd pointed out the inherent absurdity of believing that a change in the law could best be effected by violently breaking it and he had refused to take part in any such act. One or two had called him coward . . .

There was a call from downstairs. 'Are you all right, Steve?'

His mind jerked back into focus. 'Yes.'

'It's nearly a quarter past.'

He couldn't remember turning off the tap, but the water wasn't running. He washed quickly. A copy of the ten commandments of Hanburrey had been given to every student on arrival. Commandment number one: Never remember the true past, only the past we give you. But his true past demanded stronger bonds to keep it imprisoned than he'd ever been able to forge. Judith had only to call him a fighter and memory whipped him back in time to when he had chosen not to fight, but to run; memory recalled Moira, who had sought to practise every form of perversion that an ingenious mind could envisage . . .

He went downstairs and Judith came out of the kitchen, a pile of ironing in her hands. 'You're sure nothing's wrong? You seemed to be such ages.'

'I was contemplating my navel.'

'I imagine you'll find the naval programme much more rewarding . . . Hurry up, or you'll miss the beginning.'

In the sitting-room, Bob was watching a cartoon. 'Turn over to BBC Two, will you, Bob?' said Judith from the doorway.

'Why?'

'Hurry up. Steve wants to watch a programme all about old sailing ships.'

Bob made no move to pick up the remote control. 'I want to watch this.'

'Will you please do as I ask.'

'But it's my favourite programme.'

She walked to the coffee-table, picked up the remote control, and altered the programme. Introductory credits were being shown, superimposed on a scene of billowing canvas and a sea which did not look rough until foaming water swept over the lee bulwarks.

'Why can't I watch? Why's it always what he wants to see?'

'Don't be stupid.'

Bob began to cry, kicking the sofa with his heels as he did so.

'If you can't control yourself, you'd better go up to your room.'

Bob stared at Collins, a look of hatred on his tear-stained face, then he came to his feet, ran out of the room and slammed the door shut behind himself with all the force he could.

Collins said: 'You don't think we ought to let him go on watching since it was cartoons?'

'Steve, it only makes things worse to give in to him.'

'Normally, yes, but he seems to be in a bit of a state.'

'Because he's learned that that's how to get his own way with you.'

'I'm not certain that's being fair.'

'You reckon to know my son better than I do?' The moment she'd spoken, she regretted the words. Now, he was their son, not just hers. 'Oh, Steve,' she murmured. Then, as he came forward to put his arms round her: 'And we thought at the beginning that it was all so easy.'

'Nothing worthwhile is easy.'

'You sound just like the hypocrite of a maths master I had.'

'Thanks for the comparison.'

She reached up to kiss him, released herself. 'I must start the supper moving. And you must watch whatever's left of your programme after the rest of the family has done its worst.'

He sat down on the settee. For the moment there was no footage of ships and a marine historian was detailing, in a voice which soon bored because it didn't change pitch, the record and average times of passages from Europe to Australia via the Cape and Australia to Europe via the Horn. His attention wandered. 'And we thought at the beginning it was all so easy.' Bob was causing an increasing number of disagreements between Judith and himself. True, for the moment these were merely pinpricks, but pinpricks could deepen into fatal wounds . . . The historian finished and the screen showed a line of men, dressed like tramps, heaving on a halyard, water swirling around their boots. Perhaps they had been wet, cold, hungry, and exhausted, but their life had had the inestimable advantage of being simple to understand.

CHAPTER 8

They'd become quite professional, a far cry from the beginning when it had all been a game. Now, before they executed the raid, they'd made certain what were the conditions under which they'd have to operate. There was no full-time night watchman, although a guard with a dog, employed by a local security firm, checked that all was quiet at irregular intervals; the surrounding eight-foot-high chain-link fence was neither electrified nor connected to an alarm;

the two gates were secured by chains and complicated padlocks; the outside lights, on all night, were not as strategically placed as they should have been so that there was a pool of darkness over one end of the right-hand building; the windows and doors of both buildings were wired up to an alarm, but there was no direct line through to the nearest police station; the alarm system was a poorly designed one and it frequently sounded for no valid reason, which meant that those who lived within earshot would take little notice if it were set off; the mice were kept in banks of plastic cages.

They left the car a hundred yards up from the laboratory grounds; the road was mainly residential and since few of the houses had garages there were parked cars along its length and theirs was unlikely to attract any attention.

Although not a slum, it was a run-down part of West Emsley and two of the street lights by the chain-link fencing had been broken by children nearly three weeks before and had not yet been repaired; here, there was an area of shadow which gave reasonable cover. Two of them used massive bolt-cutters to cut out a square of chain-link fencing, then the other three were called along from the car. They crawled through the newly made hole and the last man used wire roughly to replace the square of chain-link.

Housebreakers of the old school boasted about the very high degree of skill their craft demanded; if given the chance, they'd recount at length how experience had honed their abilities to the point where they could break into any building without even disturbing the dust. In truth, however, if complete silence were not essential, no regard need be given to the damage caused, and the dust could be allowed to fly, strength and nerve were more important than skill when it came to actual entry. One man used a glasscutter to score the glass in the right-hand frame of a window, then he smeared the glass with glue, pressed a thick cloth on to the glue; when satisfied the cloth was fast, he smashed the end of a jemmy several times down on to it. When he pulled the cloth free, it brought with it most of the glass; the slivers which remained were easily extracted.

One of them knelt to provide a stepping-stone and the others clambered over him into the building. There was just enough light inside to confirm that there were three rows of cages, each row being three cages high. The watering, feeding, and cleaning of the mice was largely carried out mechanically. Some form of air-conditioning kept the smell reasonably low.

They split up and began to open up the cages. A few of the mice immediately scrambled to freedom, but the majority did not and had to be chivvied out of their cages. It was obvious that the task, if completed, was going to take them much longer than they'd reckoned and they suffered a growing sense of nervousness.

They'd been working for nearly an hour, and the floor seethed with frantic, squeaking animals, and a few dead ones they'd inadvertently trodden on or brushed off themselves with too much vigour—their concern for animals' liberation did not mean that they welcomed mice crawling up their legs—when a fierce light was suddenly trained on the building. They froze. Panic began to shake their minds.

The light moved from right to left, in turn focusing on each of the windows, all of which were unbroken since the one by which they'd entered was on the other side. The man nearest to the end window moved until he could peer out. He saw a guard, standing near a van, with a small portable searchlight. 'It's only Security,' he said.

They relaxed. Previous observations had shown that incident-free routine had dulled the efficiency of the middle-aged guard to the point where the most casual of checks was sufficient to satisfy him that all was well.

The light came back along the building. The man at the window jerked his head out of sight and he cursed this newfound enthusiasm. Once the light was past, he looked out again and now he realized something he should have noticed before; this was not the middle-aged guard who had always previously checked the site, but a younger man who was prepared to be far more thorough.

The guard opened the back door of the van and put the searchlight inside, picked up a torch and called out an Alsatian. He walked to the end of the chain-link, switched on the torch.

'Christ, he's checking the fence!'

Their sense of panic, very much stronger, returned. If the guard did not miss the square of replaced fencing—and could he miss it?—they were cornered. Like rats in a trap. An unfortunate simile, considering all the mice. Excitement was gone and only fear remained; suffering for a cause took on a new and wholly unwelcome connotation.

'He's found the hole!'

They were desperate to escape, yet their minds were now so muddled that none of them could decide which route to take. A mouse ran across the ankle of one of them and he shouted out, shocking the others into greater panic.

In the road, the guard reported over the van radio that there appeared to have been a break-in at the laboratory. After a thirty-second pause, he was ordered to wait for reinforcements which would be with him in minutes.

He was young, cocky, and eager to make his mark. He thought that it wouldn't do his image any harm if he went in right away with the dog and they caught the intruder, if still around. The management of the firm were always stressing the importance of individual initiative. He returned to the break in the fence, pulled the cut section free, sent the dog through and followed. When he was ten yards from the nearer building, he picked out the shattered window . . .

They ran to the far door, only to discover that it was

locked and there was no key. The dog, now immediately outside the broken window, barked rapidly, clearly a signal that it had winded intruders despite the smell of the mice. They heard an order given and the dog jumped up on to the sill, scrambled through and dropped to the floor. It hesitated, perhaps bewildered by the plenitude of targets. Then one man, whimpering with fright, began to run and the dog raced forward to seize him by the arm.

The guard, after considerable difficulty because of the height of the window, climbed inside. Like the dog, he also was surprised to find himself facing so many targets. 'Don't move,' he shouted.

One man had been immobilized by the dog and the other four had at that moment no precise thoughts of resistance. Had the guard acted carefully, continued to impose his authority by a display of self-confidence, there would have been no further trouble. But in his inexperience, he made the mistake of admitting, even if only implicitly, that he was on his own. 'Move up against the wall so as I can see you more clearly.'

One of them had panicked less than the others and he realized that the guard was alone and therefore did not have full control of the situation. He moved suddenly, reached for the jemmy, picked it up and threw it. The guard instinctively stepped back as he ducked and his left foot came down on a mouse; he teetered, then crashed.

They raced forward, wildly reacting to their panic, not really aware of what they were doing. As he tried to scramble up, they overwhelmed him, punching and kicking. The dog let go of his captive and advanced, snarling. One of the others grabbed the jemmy and swung it, to catch the dog across the muzzle; bone cracked and the dog's lower jaw fell half open, the tongue lolling sideways, yet still it came forward. A second blow caught it across the neck and felled it, a third, fourth and fifth battered it to death.

CHAPTER 9

'It's in this building,' said the detective-inspector. He made for the door, opened it, and stood aside for King to enter first.

A detective-constable who'd been making a desultory search—after all, this was the third—began to work with much greater energy; a detective-sergeant, brushing the plastic cages with dark-coloured fingerprint powder, looked up, then continued at the same even pace.

The dead Alsatian lay on the floor, an irregularly shaped patch of clotted blood stretching out from its shattered jaw. A couple of blowflies were circling round.

'It's turning out to be quite a job to get rid of this,' said the DI, pointing at the dog.

King looked around himself. 'When the guard radioed in, what details did he give?'

'Only that he'd found a break-in point in the outside fence. He was ordered to do nothing before reinforcements arrived.'

'But he went in on his own because he's been watching too much television . . . Have you been able to question him yet?'

'Only very briefly. There were five intruders—I don't yet know that it was certain all five were male—wearing dark clothes, gloves, and ski masks. No further descriptions.'

King put his right hand in his trouser pocket and jingled some coins. 'How badly injured is he?'

'Severely, but not critically. Bust ribs, extensive heavy bruising, the sight in his right eye defective but they think it'll probably recover, damage to one kidney.'

'He's lucky they didn't use the jemmy on him.' King

turned to stare at the rows of cages. 'There's no doubt their object was to release the mice?'

'None whatsoever. Half of them were loose by the time the security guard arrived. Some died, some have been recovered, but the majority have vanished. The head of the lab says they've buggered up months, maybe years, of work.'

'Then we can be certain we're dealing with an animal liberation group. No one's yet claimed responsibility?'

'No, and for my money no one will, seeing a dog was smashed to death.'

'That doesn't follow. Their logic can be impossible to understand.'

'It's not just their logic . . . We've turned up one thing, but to date it's no great help; maybe you can make something of it. The jemmy they used has RDC stamped into one end.'

King thought for a while. 'Radlington District Council,' he finally said.

'You've an idea who we could be dealing with?'

'Yes,' he answered grimly. If he'd guessed correctly, then his worst prognostications could come true. In their panic, the intruders had used brutal violence; they had learned that it could pluck success out of failure; they had tasted its perverted pleasures. This might well be the turning-point which changed them from misguided nuisances into terrorists.

A uniform PC entered and came up to them. The DI spoke to him and he hurried back outside. 'We've managed to fix up a body-bag to take the dog away in,' said the DI. 'God, the fuss and red tape because it's not a human body.'

'Make certain someone goes over it with a fine-tooth comb. There could be a trace caught up in its coat.'

'I've made all necessary arrangements.' The DI's voice expressed resentment. He was in charge of the case, even though King easily outranked him. King was not a member of the county force and therefore had no direct authority unless and until the Chief Constable gave it to him.

'I'm sure you have. Point taken,' replied King and he smiled briefly.

The DI, despite himself, smiled back. He knew from experience that when tired and frustrated, one did not worry as much as one should about protocol; especially if one was as sharp as King's reputation suggested.

'Well, there's nothing more I can do. I'd be grateful if you'd keep me posted on any developments.'

'Of course.'

'A photograph of the jemmy together with an enlargement showing the letters would be appreciated.'

'I'll get them to you as soon as possible.'

'Tell the guard I hope he soon recovers.'

'I'll do that.'

King left the building. Beyond the chain-link fence, a small group of onlookers had gathered. Satisfy their curiosity, he thought, and take them inside to see the true face of crime—the battered dog—and they'd be sickened . . . He looked up. Visible beyond the roofs of the houses, sufficiently distant for all detail to be lost, were the rolling hills which lay to the west of the town. A man who scorned sentimental symbolism, he nevertheless saw here the proof that however sordid the immediate present, there was always beauty not too far away.

Newton decided that he'd buy a Ferrari Boxer. When he won the pools. He replaced the copy of *Motor Sport* on the rack and walked towards the door of the newsagents which, owned and run by an Indian family, seemed never to shut. The young woman behind the cash desk smiled goodbye; her lustrous brown eyes made him think of bed, which made him think of Sandra.

The evening was warm but overcast and the forecast was

for heavy showers. Did it ever do anything but rain in Radlington? Why didn't the rain return to that blasted plain in Spain?

He began to walk. Radlington was a stuffy town, populated by stuffy people. They needed a trip up to Cumberland (no Cumbria for him). The winds there would blow the cobwebs out of anyone. And even if it did rain in Cumberland, it was a cleaner, more invigorating rain than that which fell in Radlington . . .

Both telephone kiosks were free and he entered the nearer one, inserted a coin, and dialled. The call was answered by Mrs King. As he waited for her to call her husband, he remembered that the last time he'd met her she'd been even more glossily turned-out than usual and could have stepped straight out of a fashion page. Trust the old bastard to pick one like her!

'What's happening?' asked King, not bothering with any social greeting.

'Nothing new, I'm afraid, sir.'

'Sitting on your arse all day?'

'Sitting? I've worn out two pairs of shoes already.'

'And I believe in fairies; the kind that aren't interested in sex . . . Listen, Reg. An animal group has pulled a job in Emsley which went wrong and they beat up a security guard and killed his dog. They left behind a jemmy on the end of which are stamped the letters RDC. Find out if that means it's likely the jemmy came from Radlington.'

'Got it.'

'If it did, ALFA's hard cell in Radlington pulled the job and that means they're blooded. Their next one could be very nasty.'

'I'll do what I can.'

'As quickly as you can.'

The call was soon over and Newton dialled a second number. As he waited, he wondered why King couldn't –

or was it wouldn't? – understand how difficult things were. The ALFA crazies worried far more about their security than a Scottish maiden about her virginity and he was finding it extremely difficult to make any progress at all. He still couldn't even be certain in his own mind whether Jeremy Lees did or did not know much of real consequence . . .

Sandra said: 'One-four-six-three-two.'

His mind abruptly switched tracks.

Lees, seated behind the wheel of his car, said: 'D'you see?'

'Of course I bloody do,' replied his companion who, in the indifferent light inside the car, looked rough-hewn, as if the sculptor had not bothered to finish the bust.

Definitely from south of the green, thought Lees. 'It's the fourth time . . .'

'You said.'

'Yet there's a phone in the house where he's living . . .'

'Can't you keep your bloody mouth shut?'

Lees gained comfort from one of his mother's sayings; a gentleman swore at hounds, not people.

The man looked at his watch. 'He's been talking for ten minutes already. It's a woman.'

'He told me he doesn't have a girlfriend.'

'You think you're his confessor?'

'No, it's just that . . .'

'You don't like him, do you?'

'That's got nothing to do with it.'

'Answer the bleeding question.'

'It's not that I actually dislike him. It's just . . . Well, we've nothing much in common.'

'That's not surprising.' The man's voice was scornful.

Lees became desperate to prove that he wasn't being a fool and that there was substance in his suspicions. 'The first call was very short. Perhaps it's that one which he doesn't want to make from the house. He stays on to talk to a girlfriend—one he's never told me about.'

'Was it the same pattern the other times—a short call and then a very much longer one?'

'Yes.'

'You saw this, each time?' The man turned and stared at Lees. 'You're sure it was two calls, one short, one long?'

'Well, I . . . I'm pretty certain.'

'Yeah? Or you'll say anything to black him?'

'That's not right. The last time, he definitely made two calls. On the previous occasions to that, I'm fairly certain but I can't swear absolutely.'

'Then you'd better find out what happens the next time.'

'I'll try, but . . .'

'But you'll bloody succeed.'

Two minutes later Newton put the receiver down, left the kiosk, and walked briskly up the road towards the crossroads.

'He lives up that way?' asked the man.

'In a house in Compton Street, which is at the back of . . .'

'You can drop me off in the Broadway.'

There was sufficient traffic to make a U-turn difficult and Lees drove to the far end of the green and then down on the north side. The lights were in his favour and he turned into the High Street, continued on for a quarter of a mile to the main shopping area where he stopped.

'Just bloody well remember this. You tell me what actually happens, not what you want to happen.' The man climbed out, slammed the door shut, and strode off. Hating him for his arrogant lack of manners, Lees watched him for several seconds before drawing away from the pavement.

CHAPTER 10

Radlington had two parks, the northern one of which was the more popular, having a large open expanse of grass. Newton walked along the central diagonal path which divided the park into two roughly equal sections and then turned on to the grass when level with a man who was cutting the grass between, and immediately around, three flowerbeds where the gang mower had been unable to go. He spoke to the gardener as he pointed at the nearest bed. 'It's all looking nice.' He had to shout to overcome the noise of the two-stroke motor. 'Especially those roses.'

The middle-aged gardener did not bother to look up.

'Would you know what their name is?'

'No.'

'I wondered if they were Charles Savoury?'

The gardener turned the mower round the end bed.

'I think, with that shade of grey, that's what they must be. Don't see them all that often, do you?'

'See 'em every working day.'

'Yes, of course.' Newton chuckled. 'By the way, back near the side gate there's a spade on the grass. I suppose it's one of yours?'

'I ain't left one anywhere.'

'It's got RDC stamped on the handle. I imagine that stands for Radlington District Council?'

'Might do.'

'So it is one of yours, then?'

'What d'you want me to do about it?'

'I was only just wondering if it had been forgotten . . .'

The gardener went to turn and found Newton in the way. 'If you ain't anything to do all day, I 'ave.'

'Sorry. Mustn't keep a man from his work, must I?' Newton smiled a goodbye, walked back across the grass to the path and then down to the main gates.

As he left the park and started along the pavement, he wondered if King was right in fearing that a watershed had been reached? Those members of ALFA whom he'd provisionally identified as belonging to the hard cell all seemed to be weak or twisted in some way and it was difficult to imagine them as terrorists. Yet history showed that fanaticism could turn weakness into strength . . . It obviously needed a far more trained mind than his to be able to judge the kind of people they might become in given circumstances.

All he knew for certain was that he'd be thankful when he could leave Radlington and return home and once more live among people who did not believe that the world could ever be made perfect, however much one tried.

Lees dialled the number. 'It's Robin,' he said, feeling, as always, both foolish and excited by the use of a nom de guerre.

'Yeah?'

He pictured the man with the rough-hewn face and south-of-the-green manners. 'He made two calls last night.'

'And?'

'The sequence was the same. A brief call and then one that lasted just short of a quarter of an hour. I did my best to count how many digits he dialled.' He waited for praise for his initiative, but here was none. 'I'm certain there were too many for the calls to have been local ones.'

'Make contact with him and find out how curious he is.'

'That won't be easy. I mean, I haven't seen anything of him recently because . . . Well, we stopped being friendly.'

'Try cuddling up to him again.' The line went dead.

He knew he was flushing heavily as he replaced the

receiver. The suggestion was a filthy one. Just because he wasn't married and didn't have a girlfriend . . .

He left and walked towards his parked car. It was easy to give orders if one were not concerned about how they were to be carried out. He'd been so piqued by Newton's betrayal of their friendship that . . . Well, he'd said several things which might have sounded rather stupid. How could he now begin to renew the friendship without making himself look a complete fool?

He unlocked the car door and settled behind the wheel. He loved driving his 309 GTi because anyone with any knowledge of cars envied him. Behind the wheel, he felt a different man.

It seemed as if the flush of pride had inspired him because he suddenly realized something; if he were right and Newton was a spy, then Newton would be so eager to renew their friendship in order to learn more about ALFA and the hard cell that he'd leap at the chance and not react with scorn. In fact, the eagerness with which he accepted an approach would be a reliable measure of his guilt.

Thirty years of development had brought to Oakley Cross all the benefits of a modern town; a system of one-way roads which increased the rate of traffic, and of accidents, and only occasionally left a driver hopelessly lost among its labyrinthine coils, supermarkets which offered quick, impersonal service instead of the slow, chatty service of the vanished family businesses, and high-rise office blocks, in which no regard had been given to such unprofitable things as proportion, in place of Georgian and Victorian houses.

In his office on Market Street, Collins stood and crossed from his desk to the single large window. He could just see the clock tower which marked the original site of the market, abolished fifteen years before in the face of progress. A new shopping centre was about to be built around the clock

tower—which had been saved from demolition by conservationists. He wondered what Oakley Cross had been like
forty years previously? Probably very similar to Radlington;
sleepy, except on market days, run by a handful of business-
men who were even richer than their enemies believed them
to be . . .

The internal phone rang. Had he prepared the projected
figures on the Berkeley Development? He replied that he'd
almost finished them and would bring them along within
the hour.

He returned to the window. Dermot Cartright was a
product of the new Oakley Cross, just as the new Oakley
Cross was a product of Cartright; they had grown together.
Cartright now had so many fingers in so many pies that
there had to be times when he'd none left with which to
wipe his nose. He'd started work as a coal merchant, reput-
edly never delivering more than nineteen hundredweight
for every ton ordered. The story was possibly true since now
he never accepted anyone's word, but always demanded
that everything be checked. Yet *Quis custodiet ipsos custodes*?
As far as it was possible to judge, Cartright had never
employed anyone to check that his checking was accurate
and honest. In fact, on one occasion the figures he'd produced had been quite contrary to those which Cartright had
expected and he'd suggested that someone else went over
them; Cartright had impatiently dismissed the suggestion
on the grounds that if he'd done the work, it was correct.
The real irony here lay in the fact that if Cartright had
known his accounts manager had a criminal record, he
wouldn't have trusted him to add two and two . . .

There'd been a time when it had been his ambition to
become as rich, powerful and influential as Cartright. Even
before he'd qualified, he'd mapped out a career in either
commerce or merchant banking which would ensure that
his income reached up beyond the mere Porsche level. He'd

begun that climb when he'd gone for a walk and seen a shot
cock pheasant dying bloodily in the snow . . . At the time,
he'd been seeing a lot of Caroline, the daughter of a wealthy
industrialist; marriage to her had offered so many worldly
advantages that it had been easy to forget that she was an
extravagant snob who kept her sexual responses in deep
freeze. After he'd joined ALFA and taken part in a couple
of local anti-shooting demonstrations, she'd dropped him
like a ton of red-hot bricks because in her milieu it was a
far greater disgrace to be anti-huntin', shootin', and fishin',
than it was to be suffering from AIDS.

Then he'd met Moira. Her sexual responses had been
born in the pit of a volcano; perhaps even in the antechamber
of hell . . . Forget your past and remember only the past we
give you, Hanburrey had repeatedly said. As time moved on,
he became less and less certain that they'd been completely
right. Only by remembering Caroline and Moira could he
now appreciate to the full what a wonderful person Judith
was; only by remembering how he'd been prepared to betray
himself by marriage in order to reach the top could he
now understand the pleasure of aiming lower and enjoying
self-honesty. Remembering his past enabled him to refute
Solon's assertion that no man could be called happy until
he was dead . . .

Lees ordered a gin and tonic. He always felt uncomfortable
in a bar because he never knew anyone else and couldn't
escape the feeling that the other customers were laughing
at his gaucherie.

'That's a quid, luv.'

The barmaid wore a cotton blouse which sculpted her
full breasts tightly enough to make it clear that she did not
wear a brassière. He picked up the glass and went over to
the table in the corner. Frequently his mother turned off the
television because a steaming love scene was working up to

its climax; he guiltily hoped she'd never realize how much he'd longed to watch on.

He sipped the drink, not really liking it, but uncertain whether it was sufficiently manly to order a sweet sherry in a bar. He checked his watch. Newton was late. Not really to be wondered at—had Newton been a Radlingtonian, he'd have been born south of the green. There was a burst of laughter from the bar and he looked across; two men were sharing a joke with the barmaid and the quality of the laughter suggested the joke had been deep blue. Dirty jokes embarrassed him.

He lit a cigarette. His mood of self-pity slowly gave way to one of slight confidence. Despite what some people might think, he was far from being a fool. He'd worked out a way of virtually making certain whether or not Newton was a spy. He'd feed Newton information which as a spy he'd have to pursue so hard that he'd forget the need for discretion . . .

Newton came through the outside doorway into the bar. As he watched him thread a way between the tables, Lees knew a bitter jealousy: why should someone else be lucky enough to find the world an easy place to live in?

'Sorry I'm late, Jerry; got caught up with a bird . . . What are you drinking?'

Lees hastily stood. 'It's my round.'

'I only argue when someone says it's mine.' He sat. 'I'll have a half of lager and if it's Foster's, tell 'em I don't want a crocodile in it.'

He didn't know what Newton was talking about. He crossed to the bar and as he waited for the busty barmaid to serve him, he decided that Newton was obviously very eager to let bygones be bygones.

As soon as he was handed the tall glass, Newton said: 'First today and may I be drowned in a butt of malmsey if that's a lie.' He drank. 'So how's the world been treating you?'

'I can't complain.'

'Then you're lucky.'

'Aren't things going very well with you?'

'I took a ticket in the local lottery and it didn't win. How can I ever smile again?' He grinned cheerfully, produced a pack of cigarettes, saw Lees was still smoking, and lit one. He chatted inconsequentially and amusingly, finished the lager. 'Drink up and I'll get the refill.'

'I don't think I want another, thanks.'

'There's a law against going into a pub and having only one drink. Same again, then, and was it a gin and tonic?'

As Newton went over to the bar, Lees wondered whether it was the other's idea to loosen his tongue with liquor; if so, it was a game two could play . . .

Twenty minutes, and two drinks later, Newton said: 'Been busy lately?'

'There has been a lot to do at the office, yes.'

'I wasn't meaning that. What about the real work?'

Lees looked round at the other tables.

'There's no one within earshot except that couple and the Last Trump wouldn't divert them.'

'One has to be so careful.'

'Sure. Careful not to overdo it . . . So now tell me, is there anything big on the horizon?'

'Well . . . The trouble is, you're not in with us.'

'Whose fault is that? I said I was keen; don't care what's on the menu so long as it's doing rather than talking. But I'm still waiting.'

'I know, Reginald, but . . .'

'You did pass on my message, didn't you?'

'Yes, I did.'

'So who did you give it to?'

Lees drank.

'Don't you trust me, Jerry?'

'Of course I do.'

'You don't make it seem like that.'

'It's just . . . We have to be extra careful now.' He slurred the words slightly, as if affected by the drink.

Newton stood. 'It's time for a refill.'

'I . . . I don't think I ought to have any more.'

'Then there's no better time to drink it.'

'But isn't it my turn to get them?'

'If you haven't been counting, I haven't been recording . . . And there's an old saying, he who's standing, does the shouting.'

Newton returned to the table and sat. He drank, wiped his mouth with the back of his hand. 'From what you've been saying, or not saying, something big's on the way?'

'I didn't say anything of the sort.'

'Relax. We're on the same side. If you've got to be extra careful, then something extra big is coming up—am I right?'

'You're . . . you're smart, Reggie.'

'Don't tell the landlady; she thinks I'm just sweet. How big a job?'

Lees spoke in a whisper. 'So big that . . .'

'That what?'

'That I'm scared.'

'It can't be that dangerous?'

'You can't go for royalty . . .' He stopped.

The astonishment in Newton's voice was genuine. 'You're aiming to hit royalty?'

'No.'

'That's what you said.'

'I didn't.'

'That's precisely so. And if that makes you scared, you're in good company. I'll light candles all the way . . . Which one of 'em is the target?'

'You've got it all wrong.'

'Not this time, I haven't.'

'I swear—'

'You've never been able to swear convincingly. Listen, I'm your friend. Tell me and the Inquisition couldn't get a whisper out of me. So who's it to be? Right up at the top, or scraping the bottom of the barrel with the imported foreigners?'

'I . . . I don't know.'

'You really don't trust me. Some friend!'

'But it's true. It may be one of the other action groups who does it and then I won't know anything more until it's over.'

'What's the method—bomb?'

'I think so.'

'By God, this'll make the headlines! . . . Look, I've got to be in on this. Tell whoever's in charge to count me in.'

'I can't.'

'Why not?'

'I shouldn't ever have mentioned it.'

'But you have.'

'If they discovered . . .'

'Who's going to tell them if you get me in on some other pretext?'

'It's impossible.'

'Only an honest politician is impossible. If you like, give me the name and I'll look him up and speak my piece with never a mention of your name.'

'I can't.'

'You know what you're doing, don't you? Working very hard at making me more and more convinced you don't trust me.'

'It's nothing like that. I just don't know who's in charge.'

'Now pull the other one.'

'Security's so tight.'

'It's never that tight. You'll have an idea.'

'I promise you I don't.'

'Then what it means is, you don't trust me and you're not really wanting to be friends again.'

'I keep telling you, it's just not like that. I do want to be friends. But I swear I haven't any idea who's in charge. Everyone now is working on a need-to-know basis.'

Newton finally accepted defeat. He spoke cheerfully, masking his angry annoyance. 'I wish I could decide if you're the father of the three monkeys or simply the most stubborn bastard I've ever met!'

Newton dialled the number and when the call was answered he said excitedly: 'Guv, we're on to a really big one. They're going for royalty with a bomb.'

'Christ!' exclaimed King. 'When?'

'I don't know.'

'Which royal?'

'I don't know any more than I've just told you.'

'Then for God's sake hurry it up.'

'I'll try, but it's not easy without raising too many suspicions.'

'I know. But now we're sitting on dynamite with the fuse lit.'

CHAPTER 11

Lees telephoned the number he'd been given. 'It's Robin. There's not the slightest doubt.'

'About what?'

The question was so unexpected—suggesting as it did that his work was not really important—that for a moment his thoughts were scattered.

'Slightest doubt about bloody what?'

He pulled himself together. 'Newton is a spy. I met him

yesterday evening and made up a story about a really big job we're going to do. He couldn't stop asking questions; kept asking who was in command and saying he wanted to meet whoever it was.'

There was a long pause.

'Are you still there?' he asked.

'Of course I'm bloody still here . . . Is there any way you can get close enough to the telephone kiosk to watch what numbers he dials?'

'Not without his seeing me.'

'Then we'll have to tackle it another way. One of you works for British Telecom—right?'

'I think Alfred does . . .'

'Haven't you yet bloody learned to control your tongue?'

He cursed himself for having used the man's real name; through congratulating himself on his own cleverness, he'd forgotten the elementary rules of security.

'Tell him to find what numbers Newton calls.'

'But how's he going to do that . . .?'

'By fixing things at the exchange, of course.'

King parked in front of Hanburrey Manor, climbed out on to the gravel, and hurried across to the portico without a glance at the scene around him. There were those who would have said that he was incapable of appreciating anything but a T26 form, but their mistake was to fail to realize it was time he usually lacked, not the ability to appreciate beauty.

He pulled the bell, in the shape of a fox's head, and waited impatiently until the heavy wooden door was opened. 'I've come to see the director. The name's Detective Chief Superintendent King.'

'Yes, sir. Will you come this way, please.'

He followed the steward across the large, panelled hall, now empty of all the furniture and hangings which had once made it welcoming and very far from the dour room it now was. A passageway took them past the blue room—a lecture hall—to the library. The steward knocked on the door, opened it, announced King.

Bowles came forward. ''Morning, Mike. You must have made very good time. I wasn't expecting you for another half-hour.'

'The traffic wasn't too heavy.' The traffic had not been light, but King had been in a hurry.

'Will you have coffee?'

'If it won't take hours.'

'You're not expecting to stay for long?'

'As short a time as possible.'

Frank, if not tactful! Bowles asked the steward to bring coffee and biscuits. He and King sat. He rested his elbows on the desk and joined his fingertips together. 'I presume you want to discuss Sanderson?'

'Yes.'

'Then it'll be best if I say right away that my answer's still the same.'

'But the facts aren't.'

'How have they changed?' He opened a silver cigarette case and brought out a cigarette which he lit.

King's voice was harsh. 'You've heard about the Emsley job where a load of laboratory mice were released, a security guard was injured, and a dog had its head smashed in?'

'Yes.'

'Chummy left a jemmy behind; stamped into the metal were the initials RDC. Radlington District Council mark most of their equipment with those initials.'

'So it was that group?'

'The odds against another animal liberation group getting hold of and using one of the council's jemmies are too small to consider. They've tasted blood. I told my lad up there to dig harder and deeper because having tasted blood, now they're ready to turn really nasty. You do realize that, don't you?'

'You talked about that the last time you were here.'

'My lad got back on to me last night. They're aiming to pull a really big job.'

'Presumably, if he's found out that much, he has a good lead on the people running the hard cell?'

'Not yet. He doesn't know whether his contact can't give him the information, or won't because he's too scared. He's working on it. In the meantime, I have to move to stop 'em. That's impossible when I don't know who they are.'

'I seem to remember you said you'd identified one member of the hard cell; it shouldn't be too difficult through him to identify the others, surely?'

'I also told you, security's bloody tight. In any case, there are definitely other hard cells in action and there's no saying which one will be assigned the next job. Unless I can identify someone at the top, or very near to there, I'm whistling the wrong tune. There's only one person can help me quickly enough—Sanderson.'

Bowles shook his head. 'I'm sorry, the answer has to remain no.'

'Listen. This big job . . . It's an assassination by bombing.'

'Bloody maniacs. But even so . . . Mike, you've got to understand my position. I can't act as a referee, balancing the pros against the cons; I can't decide that if the interests of the general public appear to override those of an individual, I should disclose details. I'm under an inviolable duty not to disclose the information you're asking me to give.'

'You don't give a damn about consequences? The people killed and maimed by a bomb mean nothing to you?'

'That's grossly unfair.'

'Life's grossly unfair, but if a man's anything in him,

when he gets the chance he does what he can to even things up.'

'Before anything else, he has to honour his duty.'

'If your superior told you it was your duty to murder a dozen people with a bomb, you'd do it?'

'There's an overriding duty not to murder, no matter who gives the order. The Nuremberg trials unequivocally confirmed that.'

'But you can't see that there's an analogous duty to save lives if it lies within your power to do so?'

'As I understand things, that isn't the case here. This bombing is merely projected so far: only one in a hundred projected crimes is ever seriously examined, only one in ten seriously examined is carried out. Further, even if this turns out to be the exception, there's no certainty that any information Sanderson can give you will help you prevent the assassination.'

'Does that mean you're still refusing to give me the information concerning Sanderson?'

'It does.'

King stood, walked over to the nearer window, head held forward in characteristic pose. As he stared out at the park, he said: 'I respect a man who honours his duty.'

'But?'

He swung round. 'That's right. There's a but. I'm going to tell you something that's classified top secret and I'm not going to insult you by warning you not to mention it to anyone. The bombers' target is royalty.'

'Christ!'

King returned to his chair, sat. 'When I forecast that the Emsley job could act as a catalyst, I'd no idea how bloody soon I was going to be proved right.'

'Do you know which of the royals?'

'No.'

'Then there are a lot of targets.'

'Which is why you have to give me Sanderson's name and address.'

Bowles lit another cigarette. 'Your contention is that because the target is a royal, my duty to divulge the information you want overrides my duty not to?'

'Of course.'

'I'm not certain that that can be right.'

'Why not?'

'Does being royal make one person inherently more important than another?'

'Are you round the twist? Of course it does.'

'Only in the scale of social values, not the scale of humanity. And even if one grants greater value, does that automatically entitle a greater degree of general protection? Surely, in fairness, the reverse should be the case? Royals are always protected by bodyguards, so they start with an enormous advantage. And although pain is pain whether you're royal or a street cleaner, if you're the former you'll have the pick of the top specialists in London . . . This means that the street cleaner's by far the more vulnerable and therefore should be afforded the greater protection. In other words, the mere fact that the target is royalty cannot logically be deduced as a reason for my breaking my duty.'

'You're a bloody Commie!'

Bowles smiled briefly. 'Only if that means that I try to get my values right.'

'You couldn't have got them more bloody wrong because you've forgotten something.'

'Probably.'

'If a street cleaner gets blown up, that's tough; if a royal gets blown up, it's also a constitutional and political crisis.'

'And, perhaps, a professional crisis for those whose job it was to prevent the assassination?'

'Are you saying that it's my own skin I'm really worried about?' King demanded loudly and roughly.

'Wouldn't you have to be a fool not to have that in mind?
. . . But no, I'm quite certain that your one overriding
consideration has nothing to do with your own interests.'

King stood. 'I'm buggered if I can begin to understand
you.'

'Maybe you're expecting too complicated a viewpoint.
I've always thought of myself as a simple man.'

'Remember who said that!' King crossed to the door.

'Mike.'

He turned the handle and swung the door open.

'Hang on.'

'What for? More left-wing balls?'

'To listen to me admit that while I'm quite certain person-
alities cannot change a man's duty, I'm not so sure that
very occasionally they may not slightly alter it. Although a
royal is no more than human, royalty is an ideal and when
an ideal is shattered everyone is hurt. It's that which makes
a royal more important than a street cleaner. So although
I won't give you Sanderson's present name and address, I
will speak to him, explain things, and ask him to get in
touch with you.'

Officially it was known as CALTU (Call Tracer Unit), but
among the engineers it was referred to as the virgin's friend.
It had been developed at the police's request after a long
succession of obscene and threatening telephone calls in
West London which had left women feeling not only frightened, but also horribly degraded.

The first CALTU had been shoe-box size and the task of
wiring it into the circuits had been one to make the engineers
curse. The third generation CALTUs were cigarette-pack
size and very simple to connect. A unit had the ability to
trace the telephone number of any national caller, provided
only that the line was held open for a minimum of twenty-
five seconds. The caller's number was transmitted to a

receiving unit—considerably larger and therefore placed where there was more room—which printed it out; the receiving unit could handle a virtually limitless amount of traffic and therefore there was no need to know the approximate times within which the call was likely to be made or to have an observer on hand to log the numbers. Because it had been held that CALTU might represent an invasion of privacy, permission of someone of the rank of divisional manager or higher had to be obtained before it was used.

Alfred Weatherby identified the circuits belonging to the two call-boxes on the south side of the green and wired a CALTU to each. Normally a man of great precision, nervousness made him work clumsily and his hands were shaking when he stuck on to each unit a square of paper bearing the forged authorization of the divisional manager. But no one took the slightest notice of him. No one ever did.

CHAPTER 12

Collins arrived home at half past six, garaged the car, and walked slowly round to the front door, enjoying the view of fields, thorn hedges, hedgerow trees and garden. Every man had his own Shangri-la and his was a moated manor house set in the middle of its own land . . . As he entered the house, Judith appeared at the head of the stairs. 'Someone's been trying to get hold of you; she rang twice and the second time I gave her your office number—did anyone get on to you there?'

'No.'

'It's obviously rather important.'

'Any idea what it's about?'

'She said she was ringing on behalf of Mr Harmsworth.'

'Harmsworth . . . Do we know anyone by that name?'

'I can't think of anyone.'

'Are you sure it wasn't Hanley?'

'Am I likely to muddle the two names?'

He grinned. 'Yes.'

'Just for that, I've a good mind not to bother with your supper.'

'Then I apologize, humbly, contritely, and . . .'

'And hungrily.' She came down the stairs. 'Is everything all right at work?'

'Not a single alarm or excursion, perhaps because Cartright is in London on some deal; buying the Albert Hall maybe.'

She kissed him.

'Where's Bob?'

'Having tea with the twins and I'm to collect him at seven . . . I tried to have a talk with him on the drive over. I asked him if he really did resent you and if so, why? He wouldn't try to explain his feelings, but just clammed up.'

'It's going to take time.'

'We've been saying that for rather a long time now . . . Steve, ought we to ask for help; maybe take him to see a psychiatrist?'

'No.'

'Why are you so adamant?'

'Because psychiatrists and children are like sugar and weedkiller; mix them up and there's an explosion.'

'That's being terribly prejudiced.'

'Just certain that most people are much better off without them.'

'It's strange you should be like this when normally you're so broad-minded. Have you had to deal with them at some time in the past?'

'No.' He remembered the resident psychiatrist at Hanburrey; a humourless man who had returned again and again to the danger of anthropomorphizing animals because nothing would convince him that his patient was not a fanatic . . .

'Come back, Steve.'

'I'm sorry.'

'I wish I could travel with you when you disappear like that.'

'Why?'

'To see what kind of country you wander into. What were you doing just then? Lining a whole row of psychiatrists up against a wall and turning a machine-gun on them? . . . Steve, do you really think that before too, too long Bob will accept my being married to you? You don't say that just to try to stop me worrying?'

'I'm certain he will. Talk to any of your beloved psychiatrists and he'll tell you that some resentment is natural.'

'I don't love them, I just think that there are times when they can probably help . . . Just suppose . . . Look, there must be times when a child doesn't become reconciled to a step-parent. If it was like that with us, you wouldn't turn against me, would you?'

'Good God, no!'

'That can happen.'

'Not to us.'

'Why not?'

'Because we're wonderfully unique.'

She laughed. Then she said: 'Because of having to fetch Bob, it won't be much before eight when we eat. If you like, you've time to mow the lawn.'

'I don't like.'

'But you agreed at breakfast that it needed doing; leave it much longer and you'll be making hay.'

'I'm pretty tired. I'll do it tomorrow.'

'I seem to remember that that's what you said yesterday when I offered to delay the meal.'

'The truth is, I'm waiting to see if old Farmer Jones's cows break loose and graze the grass first . . . Let's celebrate by having a drink?'

'What is it this time; your laziness?'

'The fact that today's Friday and there's no more office until Monday.'

The telephone rang while they were having supper. Judith sat nearer to the door and she stood. 'If it's Mary,' he said, 'tell her we're eating and will she ring back later for her half-hour session of slander.'

'And she thinks you're such a charming man!'

She left, to return soon. 'It's the lady with the call from the mysterious Mr Harmsworth.'

In the hall, he picked up the telephone receiver. 'Collins speaking.'

A woman asked him to hold on and he waited. 'Patrick Bowles here, Steve.'

Such were the strange tricks that a mind could play that for a brief moment he failed to identify the name. Then he did. 'Why?' he demanded harshly.

Bowles incorrectly judged the import of the question. 'I thought it would probably be best if I assumed a false identity and then no conclusions could be drawn by anyone else.'

'Why have you got in touch with me?'

'Because I have to tell you something.'

Acting instinctively, he carefully closed the door between the hall and the kitchen.

'I expect you remember Detective Chief Superintendent King?'

'I'm hardly likely to have forgotten him.'

'He's been on to me more than once, asking me to give him your present name and address.'

'Have you?'

'Of course not.'

He relaxed. King would not be coming to Brecks Cottage . . . He'd never told Judy the truth. For a while after meeting her he had not been certain he was in love and so there'd been no need to speak; when he'd accepted that he was, he'd been too afraid that he'd lose her to a local cricket hero if he admitted that he was a convicted criminal whose criminal associates had threatened to murder him because they believed he'd betrayed them; by the time they were married, he'd realized that he could never speak without proving himself to have been a liar and a deceiver. 'What does he want?'

'As you've probably read, one or more hard cells within ALFA up north have been committing acts of violence and the last one resulted in serious injury to a guard. It's generally accepted that when a pressure group turns to violence, whether in pursuit of, or as a consequence of, its aims, such violence will be on an increasing scale and this means that King became reasonably convinced that ALFA's next job would be an even more serious one. Unfortunately, he's learned he was right. An act of terrorism is being planned which will have disastrous consequences and lead to the deaths and serious injuries of a number, perhaps a large number, of people. To avoid this happening, he wants to ask you to help him.'

'How am I supposed to be able to do that?'

'By telling him everything you know about ALFA and in particular by identifying those in command of the sections which have turned to acts of violence.'

'No.'

'Innocent lives are at stake.'

'I said no.'

'Naturally, I understand that ties of loyalty held you silent at the time of the trial. But don't you think that the

present circumstances do release you from that loyalty?'
Bowles was very aware that, remembering all he'd said to
King, his words were laced with hypocrisy.

'No.'

'The meeting could, of course, be arranged to take place
on neutral ground, well away from your home.'

He knew a momentary hysterical desire to laugh. Bowles
sounded like a pompous bureaucrat. 'You said you hadn't
given my name or address. If I refuse to go on meeting him,
are you going to give them to him?'

'Certainly not.'

'Right. Then I refuse to meet him, any time, anywhere.'

'You wouldn't like to think it over? As I said, it is a very
serious situation.'

'I can think it over from now until the end of time and
my answer will still be no.'

'Very well. The final decision has to be yours and yours
alone.' He paused, then changed the subject. 'How are
things working out for you?'

'They were working fine until you phoned.'

'I can assure you that nothing will change through any
action of mine. Good luck, Steve, and goodbye.'

He replaced the receiver. His hands were moist with
sweat and he rubbed the palms down the sides of his
trousers. Would the past ever recede sufficiently far to
disappear out of sight?

He returned to the dining-room. Judith said: 'I put your
plate in the oven to keep warm.'

He used a cloth to take out the plate and carry it through
to his place at table. He began to eat.

'So who is Harmsworth?' she asked.

He looked up. 'Who's who?'

'The person with whom you've just been talking at some
length.'

He answered quickly. 'Just one of the blokes at work.'

'But you didn't recognize the name when I first mentioned it.'

'He's new.'

'He was obviously very keen to talk to you.'

'He has a problem.'

'A very pressing one, presumably?'

At the time, he failed to attach any significance to the tone of voice in which she'd spoken.

He yawned as he looked across at the small carriage clock which had belonged to Judy's grandmother and which now stood on the top shelf in the small alcove on the right-hand side of the fireplace in the sitting-room. 'Shall we make tracks for bed?'

'If you like,' she answered.

'A fairly early night would be some insurance against another early morning start from Bob – although he should have tired himself out with the twins. He was much less abrasive when he got back, wasn't he? Maybe if he had a five-mile walk every day, all our problems would be solved.'

'That's not funny.'

He looked at her. 'It wasn't meant to be; at best, facetious . . . Is something wrong, sweet?'

'You've no idea?'

'How could I have?'

'By remembering that when you went to the phone during supper and discovered who was calling, you shut the door from the hall into the kitchen so I couldn't hear what you had to say.'

'What in the hell makes you think I did that?'

She said pityingly: 'Are you so preoccupied you've clean forgotten I put your meal in the oven? When I went into the kitchen, I couldn't help see you'd shut the door.'

'I didn't do that on purpose. I was fidgeting with it and

when it clicked shut, I just didn't bother to open it again until I'd finished.'

'I see . . . Who's Harmsworth?'

'I told you earlier. He's a new bloke at the office.'

'And he has a problem which he wants you to help him with and so his secretary . . . I take it that the woman is his secretary?'

'Yes.'

'She not only works for him during the day, but also at night? Is she what one euphemistically calls a very personal secretary?'

'I don't know what his private arrangements are.'

'Whatever they are, you certainly didn't expect to have to become involved in them, did you?'

'What are you getting at now?'

'I'm suffering from that irritatingly feminine trait, curiosity. Before you shut the door, you said: "Why have you got in touch with me?" You sounded very shocked. Obviously you hadn't expected him to call you here.'

'All that was happening was, I couldn't understand why he didn't wait to talk to me until we were at the office.'

'Who is he?'

'Harmsworth. Why do you keep on and on?'

'If I ring up your office on Monday and ask to speak to Mr Harmsworth, will they know whom I mean?' She studied his face. 'I gather that they won't.' Her voice was dull.

She undressed in silence—she had not spoken since leaving the sitting-room—climbed into bed and picked up a paperback from the bedside table; she opened this, but read no more than a couple of lines before she put it down. She waited until he was in bed, then said: 'The night before my first marriage, my mother said she could give me only one advice about marriage that wouldn't, sooner or later, be proved hopelessly wrong; that was, never sleep on an unanswered question. Are you having an affair? Has Bob made things so difficult . . .'

'Christ, no! How could I?'

'Easily.'

'When I'm married to you?'

'I've never heard that marriage raises an insuperable barrier.'

'Mine does because I love you.'

She reached under the bedclothes and gripped his left hand. 'You really mean that?'

'I've never meant anything more.'

'Then prove it.'

Later, as she lay snuggled up to him, she said: 'I was so scared.'

'Why?'

'Because . . . because of what happened tonight, because of the trouble Bob keeps being, because of what happened with Madge and Roy.'

'For Pete's sake, what have they got to do with anything?'

'You were all for staying a weekend with them when they went house-sitting until I told you they'd be near Wem. And when we drove down from the Lake District last summer, you wouldn't go to Hodnet. So when that woman phoned you twice earlier on and the third time you were so worried, and you seemed to shut the door to prevent me hearing what you said . . . I became frightened she was someone you knew . . . knew very well and who lives near Wem and Hodnet.'

'And they say women think more logically than men! There's no one else in Shropshire or in any other county, north, east, south, or west.'

'I don't know what I'd do if you went off with someone else.'

'You'll never have to make that discovery.'

She kissed him, ran her forefinger around his mouth.

'There isn't anyone called Harmsworth in your office, is there?'

He hesitated. 'No,' he finally admitted.

'Then who was she?'

'A genuine secretary and quite certainly not one of a very personal persuasion.'

'Genuine secretary to whom?'

'A man called Patrick Bowles.'

'Who's he?'

'Someone I once knew, but didn't expect to hear from ever again.'

'Is he going to cause trouble?'

'No way.'

She waited, then said: 'Are you going to tell me all about it?'

'Would you mind very much if I don't just yet?'

'I . . . I suppose not. But you do promise me you're not in any sort of trouble?'

'I do.'

'And there's not another woman?'

'Not even the vague possibility of one.'

'It's just me you love?'

'Didn't I prove that a minute ago?'

'Yes. But you'll need to keep reminding me.'

CHAPTER 13

As he waited for King to come to the phone, Bowles tapped on the desk with the fingers of his free hand. His secretary came in with some papers; she crossed to the desk and put them down. 'One new entry and two memos from the Home Office that are WPB fodder.'

'Thanks, Anne.'

As she left, he began to read the papers. A brief glance
was all that was necessary to check that both memoranda
were as unimportant as she'd said; he scrumpled them up
together and threw them into the cane wastepaper-basket.
He carefully read through the E7 form, which was always
sent to him ahead of a new entrant's arrival. Wychley
Station at 1200 hours on the 23rd. So on that day he'd drive
the thirty miles and pick up Paul Arthur Baring. On the
drive back, he and Baring would between them decide on
Baring's new name. Once at the Manor, only the new name
would ever be used. In this way, only he or Baring could
ever betray Baring . . .

'Sorry to keep you,' said King, sounding anything but
apologetic.

'I've spoken to Sanderson.'

'When and where's the meeting?'

'He refuses to see you.'

'He bloody can't. Didn't you explain the situation?'

'I laid it straight down the line. He still refused.'

'Shit! . . . Look, suppose I could obtain permission to
pass on the fact that the target's royalty?'

'In my estimation, that wouldn't make a scrap of difference.'

'You don't think it's possible that he's patriotic?'

Bowles smiled briefly at the question since, by inference,
it made it plain that King believed him to be a rabid
republican. 'However patriotic, I think he'll be more concerned with his own life. It's understandable.'

'Not by me.'

'He's married and has a stable home. Let you back into
his life and how much would he lose?'

'All I want is information.'

'On which you'd act. Who ever knows beforehand where
the ripples of any action are going to end?'

'Start worrying about that sort of crap and all you're fit

for is sitting on your arse with your hands over your eyes . . .
All I need is a name. Pull out the top man and the rest'll
collapse like a pack of cards.'

'Will they?'

'I know the type. Without a leader to kick 'em into line,
they're no more than a disorganized bunch of misfits.'

Bowles made no comment.

'Ask him again. Force him to understand how much is at
stake.'

'I've done all I can. I assure you that there's absolutely
no point in getting back on to him.'

'You refuse even to try?'

'On the grounds that it can only be a complete waste of
time. He's defending his own nest.'

'Bloody fouling it, you mean. And you won't give me his
name and address?'

'No.'

King muttered an ill-tempered goodbye, rang off.

Bowles knew that he was in the right. Yet events could so
easily prove that to be in the right was to be tragically wrong.

Weatherby packed the strips on which were printed the
telephone numbers into a stout brown envelope; he ad-
dressed this to Robin Smith. He told his wife he was going
out to the pub for a pint, at which she complained bitterly
at the waste of money. She was a heavily built woman with
a face that would never launch even a single dinghy and
she despised him.

He walked to the small tobacconist and sweet shop, run
by an elderly, arthritic man of seventy, who wasn't worried
about how little profit the business made because he welcomed the contacts with customers. Weatherby handed him
the envelope, asked for a pack of Gold Cut, paid for both
and left, only too thankful to have got rid of the evidence.

*

Lees collected the envelope from the tobacconist and drove home. He greeted his mother, poured out two sherries, dutifully listened to her latest complaints, then said he must go upstairs and do some work on his computer before preparing dinner.

He'd already composed a program so that now all he had to do was put the two floppy discs into the drive and feed into the computer all the groups of numbers he'd just received. He had a natural gift for computing which, allied to a sharp, numerate intelligence, made him a skilled and fast programmer and operator.

Twenty-three minutes after he had started work, he had a list of fifty-six groups which had been dialled more than once. He printed them out, then entered a command to sort out those numbers which had been dialled more than twice. Now there were nine groups of which four were local. He printed out the five non-local numbers. He had a dialling code booklet and this showed that of the five numbers, two were London ones, one was from Cardiff, one from Manchester, and one from Stermthwaite.

He dialled his contact and passed on his findings.

Weatherby had fervently hoped that he wouldn't be called upon to do anything more, but he had been. Even the fact that his requested identification of five numbers could surely only appear to be a legitimate one wasn't enough to prevent his being so scared that his stomach rebelled.

'I've got them for you,' said the woman who worked in regional directory inquiries. She read out four names and addresses. 'The fifth number's ex-directory. You'll have to get special clearance to have that one identified, of course.'

'Couldn't you . . .'

'No, love, I couldn't. Not if you was to offer me a fortnight in Madeira all alone with you.'

He thanked her, rang off, stared at the four names and addresses he'd written down. Would one of these go to prove Reginald Newton a spy?

Lees was ordered to study the telephone numbers again to see if he could find any connection between the ex-directory one and any of the others. He knew the answer without having to check further. On each occasion, the Stermthwaite number had been called immediately after the ex-directory one. That fitted the presumed pattern that Newton made a brief official call and then a long private one.

Stermthwaite lay to the east of the Seascale/Whitehaven road, slightly nearer to the mountains than the coast. On a fine day—and there were usually a few each year—the mountains looked close enough to touch; on a rainy day they frequently disappeared from sight. The village was noted for two things, the salmon in the fast-flowing Alder which ran through the centre and, just beyond the northern boundary, on the edge of a farmyard, Oppoderma's Stone, traditionally the rock on which Oppoderma had stood when he had called upon the local peasants to mend their notoriously immoral ways. He had always been a man of boundless optimism.

Blackwood parked next to a dark blue Jaguar V12, climbed out of his Montego, brushed his moustache with crooked forefinger, and crossed to the door of the saloon bar. In his natty tweed suit, he looked like a man who would have great difficulty in selling a second-hand car.

The pub had not been modernized and such was the perversity of human nature that because of this it drew a lot of custom away from others in the area which had updated their images in order to attract the young. It was several minutes before he was able to order a Scotch and soda and a further ten before one of the two women serving behind the bar showed herself willing to accept a drink and to chat.

'What name did you say?' she asked.

'The Murrays. I used to know the family back in the old days and then lost touch with 'em; all I've been able to find out is that they've maybe moved to this area.'

'Can't say I've heard of 'em, but I've not been long here myself. Beryl might know.'

He waited. She served a couple of customers, then spoke to her companion, returned. 'There's the Murrays what live down the road. Beryl says they've been here for years.'

'It must have been a long time since my friends moved. Does this Murray have ginger hair?'

'Can't say. Like I said, it's Beryl who knows about 'em.'

'Maybe she could have a word?'

Beryl came down the bar to where he sat. 'You're asking about the Murrays?' She was thin, middle-aged, and her light brown eyes were constantly on the move; he placed her as the publican's wife, sharp of mind and tongue and not easily swindled.

He explained, in greater detail this time, how he and the Murrays had been good friends, but he'd moved south and lost contact; then he'd heard that they'd moved years ago to Stermthwaite, or somewhere near there, and since he was up in the area, he'd decided to try and look them up . . .

'He's not got red hair,' she said, as she polished a glass. 'Not got much hair at all, but what there is is grey.'

'Is his wife not very tall and a little plump?'

She nodded, unconcerned by the vagueness of the description.

'And they've a daughter?'

'There's two; one of 'em's married and lives in Wigan, or somewhere like that.'

'And the other—is she a good-looker?'

'Depends what you fancy, doesn't it?'

He smiled. 'From the way you're talking, she's not married yet?'

'No, but she's a young man and I hear they're planning on marrying as soon as they can.'

'I suppose he works locally?'

'That's right. In the police.'

Newton's landlady was a sparrow of a woman, never still; she often said that they'd have a job to keep her in her coffin long enough to screw the lid down. She knocked on his bedroom door. 'Reg, the telephone's for you.'

He stepped out on to the landing. 'Who is it, Mrs P.?'

'A lady. She didn't give a name.'

His immediate thought was that the call concerned Sandra and something terrible must have happened because when he'd given her the telephone number she'd promised only to use it in a real emergency. He found it difficult to breathe freely and as he crossed to the head of the stairs, he visualized a succession of catastrophes.

He hurried down the steep stairs to the phone, picked up the receiver. 'Yes?' His voice was strained.

'Is that Reginald Newton?'

He didn't recognize the woman's voice. 'Who's that? What's happened?'

'I thought you might like to come along and have a chat with some friends who want to meet you.'

His relief was so great that momentarily he was light-headed. Sandra wasn't hurt, this was someone from ALFA. Almost certainly, he was at last about to be accepted as a member of the hard cell. 'That sounds a great idea. When d'you suggest?'

'What's wrong with now?'

'No reason I can think of.' It momentarily occurred to him that her tone had been almost teasing; only later did he pause to wonder why this should be. 'Where shall I meet you?'

'Walk to the end of Summers Road and I'll pick you up there in my car.' The connection was cut.

As he replaced the receiver, he knew a sense of satisfaction. Thanks to all his long and boring time in Radlington, it looked as if he were finally about to strike gold. Very soon now he'd have names, then he could quit the town with its air of seedy respectability and return to Cumberland where the wind blew fresh and 'them old boogers' meant friends, not enemies.

Mrs Prideaux had not returned to the sitting-room, but was by the hall-stand, ostensibly rearranging the hanging coats and mackintoshes. He decided to satisfy her curiosity. 'I'm going out for a bit.'

'It'll do you a world of good!'

'I won't be back late.'

'You enjoy yourself and I'll not bolt the front door . . . Maybe going to the cinema?'

'It's a thought.'

'Don't forget that there's usually something on at the Lyceum.'

'I think it's a disco evening this week.'

'I expect you enjoy dancing?'

'Only if it's the old-fashioned kind where you get the chance to hug your partner.'

She called him wicked, but thoroughly approved of his answer; a romantic, she had been worried by his apparent lack of any girlfriends.

The evening had been fine when he'd returned to the house, so he didn't bother to take his mackintosh from the stand. He left the house, went down the stone steps— cleaned every morning except Sunday—and turned left. A quick walk brought him to the end of Summers Road. There was not much traffic and he was able to watch each approaching car. Some three minutes after his arrival, a black Rover slowed to draw up alongside him. The front passenger window wound down and the woman driver, leaning across the passenger seat, said: 'Hullo, Reg.'

The street lighting was good enough to illuminate her face. She was reasonably young—by which he meant not more than a couple of years older than himself—and strikingly attractive with jet black hair, an oval face, and lustrous eyes which he thought were blue. Her eyes seemed to be sparkling with some inner excitement . . .

'Aren't you getting in?'

He opened the passenger door and sat.

'We'd better introduce ourselves, hadn't we? You're Reg; I'm Moira.'

'Hi, Moira.' There was a subtle hint of perfume in the car. For reasons which he wouldn't have begun to clarify, despite himself he began to imagine a night of excitement . . .

The car drew away from the pavement. She said: 'You must be the strong, silent type.'

'I was thinking.'

'What about?'

'I was wondering where we're going?'

'You can't find anything more interesting than that to think about?'

Surprised by the archness of her tone, he looked at her. Her mouth was slightly open, as if she were breathing much more rapidly than usual; seen in profile, her expression was one of excitement. Yet it was difficult—if highly flattering —to believe that she'd taken one look at him and suffered an overwhelming passion.

'More boring thoughts?'

'I'm afraid so.'

'And yet when I first saw you standing on the pavement, I said to myself, there's a man whose thoughts would have any girl worried.'

'Did you now?'

'Yes, I did so!' she replied mockingly. 'So maybe you're not telling me the truth. Maybe your thoughts aren't all that innocent.'

'That could be.'

'If you were truthful, d'you think I'd blush?'

'I don't suppose you blush that easily.'

She chuckled; a throaty, intimate chuckle. 'Tell me, Reg, what do you suppose it would take to make me blush?'

'I'm not such a fool as to answer that question.'

'Why not?'

'If I suggest too little, you'll be annoyed, if I suggest too much, you'll be outraged.'

'I like being outraged.'

Keep your feet firmly on the ground, Reginald Newton, he told himself. If it's being offered that freely, there'll be a catch. And catch or no catch, RN is not in the market any longer.

'D'you like Radlington, Reg?'

He was glad to be given the chance to move to neutral ground. 'It's all right.'

'You don't sound enthusiastic.'

'There's not all that much to do,' he answered automatically.

'That means you haven't anyone nice to do it with. We'll have to find someone who'll keep you amused, won't we?'

The neutral ground had been cut from under his feet.

'Before I saw you, I was expecting to meet a middle-aged man who'd bore me with all his marriage troubles . . . Have you got any troubles?'

'Thousands.'

'One of which is, you've not been having any fun. So far.'

Anyone as sexily attractive as she wasn't going to go short of men unless she wanted to; yet here she was, making a play for him. He'd known men boast that they'd made it the first night, but he'd always dismissed them as boastful liars; was she going to show him that they hadn't necessarily been so? And where was he going to find the strength of will to resist, however tempting . . .?

They passed the last house and entered the countryside; glad to have something other than her to occupy his mind, he concentrated on memorizing their route. She put down the indicator and they turned left into a narrow lane. Almost immediately they reached crossroads, where they turned right, then left again. He was, he thought, going to have one hell of a job memorizing this route if the lanes continued to imitate a maze.

'You don't have to worry about what time you get back, do you?' she asked.

'There's no sweat on that score.'

'So after we've met our friends and had a bit of a chat, we two might go somewhere?'

He ignored the question. 'Who are we meeting?'

'Just friends. It won't take long. There'll be plenty of time afterwards.'

'Sounds great.'

They passed a sign naming the village they were entering and he was able to read it; Great Oursley. Now he could place them exactly.

'You've gone all quiet again. You are the strong, silent type!'

'I do my weight-lifting every morning.'

'And in the evening?'

'I put the weights down.'

She chuckled.

Like a cat which had found a saucer of cream, he thought. For his money, almost all the people in ALFA were slightly cracked, but she was acting as if . . . As if she were a crazy whore, was the only comparison which came to mind immediately.

They passed a church and then were once more in open countryside. On a bend, the headlights picked out the gleaming eyes of a herd of Friesians; a quarter of a mile further on there were trees on either side, the top branches of which met overhead to form a tunnel.

'Do you know where we are?' she asked.

'Haven't a clue,' he lied.

'We're almost there. Are you excited?'

'Should I be?'

'Depends how hard you're thinking about what happens afterwards.'

'Couldn't think any harder.'

She chuckled once more.

They slowed, turned through a gateway with curved brickwork and wrought-iron gates and entered a hundred-yard-long drive, at the head of which was a house which, by headlights, looked large and rather ugly. They rounded a circular raised flowerbed and went down a side drive which brought them to a courtyard at the back of the house.

She switched off the engine. Her fingers rested on his left hand and, as if by chance, her thumb just reached his thigh; she leaned sideways so that her face came close to his.

He tried not to move too quickly as he opened the door and climbed out on to the cobbled surface. He wasn't too certain how close he'd been to responding to her advances. She generated more electricity than a nuclear power station.

'Follow me. Hang on, if you like; I won't shout for help.'

For the first time he experienced disquiet rather than guilty excitement. There was definitely something very wacky about her. Instinct told him to cut and run even if he couldn't divine what was going on. But if he did that he would lose a lead for which he'd been working for weeks . . .

She opened an outside door. 'Give me your hand.'

'Why?'

'The lights aren't working. But dear me—a big, strong,

healthy man like you, scared of holding hands! Don't panic. I promise not to do anything you wouldn't want your sister to know about.'

He had never found it easy to accept mockery. He took hold of her hand. Immediately, she began to rub her fore-finger against the palm of his hand. He tightened his grip to try to stop her.

She laughed, turned, and leaned back and brushed his cheek with her lips. 'I think you're just putting on an act, Reg!' Then she straightened up and stepped inside, pulling him after her.

The moon was in its first quarter and the sky was cloudy so that very little light came through the window, but she led the way without any hesitation. Like a cat, came to his mind. They passed into a passage and went along this for several paces, then turned into a room. She stopped, put her arms round him, and kissed him with open mouth and exploring tongue as she pressed her body against his and moved it.

A man's mind could be filled to overflowing with good intentions, he thought wildly, but a woman's body could scatter them to the four winds. His right hand cupped her breast. She made a low, animal noise at the back of her throat as she began to fondle him. He reached down to the hem of her skirt . . .

Abruptly, she pulled free. 'Now!'

An overhead light was switched on.

He stood in a kitchen that was not in use to judge from the bare shelves, working surfaces, and central table. One of the two windows was partially boarded up. An empty house, abandoned or waiting for renovation into flats? . . . There were two doorways, the one by which they'd entered and another in the opposite wall and through this latter had come two men, small crowbars in their hands. He moved and for the first time saw her face in full light; she looked as if in the grip of an ecstatic passion . . . They'd identified him as a spy and were now determined to kill him. He'd little hope in a straight fight and his only chance was to assert his authority. 'I'm a police officer. Put those bars down.'

They were unsettled by this order from a man who, so they had believed, would be frightened to the point of helplessness.

'Don't be silly, now. Put the bars down.'

They lowered the crowbars. He'd got them! he thought. Frightened by the action they'd nerved themselves to take, they were subconsciously grateful for a good reason not to take it . . . 'Just relax and take things quietly and there won't be any trouble. The house is surrounded. Now, put the bars down on the ground and step back . . .'

'You fools,' she shouted. 'There's no one outside. Go in and get him.' She moved so unexpectedly that he had not the time to react. She grabbed the crowbar from the man nearer to her, swung it, and caught him across the side of his face. As he staggered sideways, a piercing pain said his cheekbone had been fractured.

His authority as well as his cheekbone had been shattered. So now his only hope was to break clear before they could catch him . . . A second blow, landing near the first, knocked him off balance and heightened his agony to screaming point. Blindly, he struggled to regain his balance, but two more blows, one to the top of his head, one to his neck, sent him sprawling. He heard her shouting at them to hit harder and wondered what kind of a woman she could be. Just before he lost consciousness, he seemed to see Sandra at a distance and she was trying to tell him something, but tragically he couldn't understand a single word . . .

CHAPTER 14

Betty looked across the room. 'Do stop fidgeting.'

'I wasn't,' King replied.

'That's the umpteenth time you've looked at your watch. What's the panic?'

'I'm expecting a phone call.'

'Judging by your behaviour, from a blonde.' She spoke lightly. She was confident that she'd never lose him to any blonde, brunette, or redhead. Unless, of course, she wanted to.

'It's someone who should have phoned through an hour ago.'

'The usual caller?'

He nodded.

'What's he up to?'

'Risking his neck.'

'How?'

'Undercover work.'

She knew that that was as much as he'd tell her; ready to share many details of his police life, there were yet some he would not. She changed the subject. 'There's a fashion show at Mundy's on Saturday. I thought I might go to it.' She was not surprised to note that he was not listening. Fashion shows were hardly his scene.

King, seated behind his desk, looked up at the DC who was dressed in polo-neck shirt and jeans. 'Has there been any word from Reg?'

'Not so much as a hullo, Guv. D'you think something's wrong?'

'Damned if I know. Pass the word that the moment there is news, I want to hear it bloody fast.'

'Will do.'

King watched the DC leave, picked up a pencil and fiddled with it. Logically, one missed telephone call wasn't enough to sound the alarm bells, yet Newton had never before broken a schedule and instinct was telling him that something was very wrong. He could do one of two things; admit that intuition could be bloody wrong and wait to see what happened, or accept that intuition could often be right and send someone in to start asking questions. If there really were cause for worry, waiting could be fatal for Newton; if there weren't, sending a man in could blow the gaffe and that would be the end of any further undercover work . . .

The loneliness of command. Share a decision which went wrong and share the blame; but only he could make this decision and only he would stand charged by the consequences . . . Surely, his decision had to be made in the light of the possibility that a really big job was being planned? In the past, the assassination of royalty had started a war; who could guess what calamity another such assassination might bring? So one man's safety didn't count for very much when the stakes were so high. Except, of course, to that one man . . .

On Saturday morning King drove into the courtyard and his reserved bay; he didn't believe rank necessarily made one man better than the next, but he was convinced that it entitled him to park without any hassle.

The duty DC saw him pass the doorway of the general room and followed him into his office. 'There's been an outside call, sir, which you need to know about. Miss Sandra Murray rang in about twenty minutes ago.'

'Reg's fiancée. What's she want?'

'To ask where Reg is.'

King slumped down in the chair behind his desk. 'So she hasn't heard from him either?'

'Not a word and it was her birthday yesterday.'

He said hopefully: 'He could have forgotten.'

'But almost certainly didn't. He posted a birthday card on Wednesday morning, which reached her yesterday, and in it he said he'd be phoning in the evening.'

King recognized that the suggestion had been a stupid one. A man in love and not yet married remembered the anniversary of everything, right down to the time as well as the date of the first kiss; it was only after his marriage that he learned a sense of proportion. He drummed on the desk with his fingers. He was left with no alternative course of action. 'Send Frank up Radlington to find out what's happened.'

Frank Grafton looked younger and a whole generation more innocent than he was and women were inclined to think he needed mothering; a misconception of which he often took full advantage.

Mrs Prideaux invited him into her house and offered him tea or coffee. She left him in the front room, returning with a tray on which were two cups of instant coffee, sugar, milk, and a plateful of chocolate digestive biscuits. He stood, took the tray and then, once she was seated, held it for her to help herself. She was further charmed by such good manners.

After a while he brought the conversation round to Newton.

'To tell the truth,' she said, 'I have become a little concerned about him not returning.'

'Because you expected him back before now?'

'Well, of course I did. I mean, the last thing he said on Wednesday night was that he wouldn't be late back.'

'You must have been worried, then, by Thursday morning?'

'Not really . . . Well, you know as well as me that things are different now from what they used to be. The young have their fun as they always did, but now they don't seem to bother about other people knowing they're having it.'

'He was out with a woman?'

'The telephone call was from one.'

'Did she give her name?'

'Not to me.'

'Did you know he had a girlfriend?'

'He's never mentioned one. But from the way he was talking, he hardly knew her and wasn't really expecting to hear from her.'

He wondered if he should ask to search Newton's bedroom, in the very slight hope of finding some clue to what was happening, but decided that to do so could only arouse Mrs Prideaux's curiosity to a much higher, and therefore potentially harmful, pitch than his visit had done. 'Well, I guess he's just enjoying himself. Will you tell him when he gets back that I'm sorry to have missed him?'

Since it was Saturday, the bank was operating a reduced service and the senior member of staff present was the assistant manager. Grafton produced his warrant card. 'I need to know one or two things about Reginald Newton's account.'

'So Mr Bottomly said.' The assistant manager was a tall, thin man who valued a precise routine above pearls and who understood a balance sheet far better than his fellow humans. 'I'm surprised that I have to point out that without a court order I am forbidden to give you any details about any client's account.'

'Yeah, I do know that. And I can go off and get an order. But that'll take time and in this case we maybe haven't any. Reg Newton's missing and this could mean he's in trouble. If he is, we need to find him very quickly.'

'I don't see how it can help you to be given details of his account.'

'If he's been in the habit of drawing money regularly and hasn't done so in the immediate past, that'll tell us a lot.'

'Then you're not asking for actual figures?'

'Just the pattern.'

The assistant manager thought for a moment, then said slowly and with reluctance: 'You've assured me it's important, so I suppose that in the circumstances it's permissible for me to divulge certain general details. But, mark this, nothing specific.'

'Agreed,' replied Grafton, wondering if a pin jammed into the other would release some of the pomposity.

The assistant manager used the intercom to give an order. They waited. They had nothing in common and their conversation was desultory; before long it virtually ceased.

A middle-aged woman brought them a sheet of paper which she put on the desk, then left. The assistant manager read what was printed on the paper, checked a calendar, looked at Grafton. 'Over the past six weeks, Mr Newton has withdrawn a certain sum of money each Friday; in four of the six weeks, he has drawn a further sum on one of the other days.'

'What about yesterday?'

'There was no withdrawal.'

'Shit!'

The assistant manager pursed his lips at this display of vulgarity.

Maggie Bowles stepped into the sitting-room and said to her husband, who was slumped in an armchair: 'Pat, there's someone to see you.'

'What's that?' he asked thickly.

'I thought you particularly wanted to watch that programme?'

'I wasn't asleep.'

'No, dear; just contemplating eternity. Shall I bring Mr King in here?'

'King!' He jerked himself upright. 'What the devil's he doing here?'

'I haven't asked and even if I had, I'm quite sure he wouldn't have answered. He's looking even more bad-tempered than when I last saw him all those years ago.'

'It's the nature of the beast.'

Did the blasted man never give up? wondered Bowles, as he waited.

King followed Maggie into the room. 'I called in at the Manor, but they said you were at home.'

Bowles was his usual polite self. 'Nice to see you again. You'll have some coffee? Or shall we declare the clocks slow and have a drink?'

'I haven't the time.'

Maggie, who was now standing behind King, raised her eyebrows to express her opinion of his rude refusal. She lowered her eyebrows, said: 'Then if you're happy to be as you are, I'll leave you to it.'

As soon as she'd shut the door, King said fiercely: 'I have to have Sanderson's name and address.'

Bowles sighed. 'Mike, we've been over this again and again. Can't you accept that I'm not going to give you the information unless he agrees to my doing so and at the moment there's no chance of that happening? I'm sorry, but I'm just not prepared to betray my duty . . .'

'For God's sake, man, climb down out of the pulpit.'

Bowles flushed.

'The lad I infiltrated into ALFA has disappeared.'

Bowles, who had been standing, sat.

'It's looking nasty, but we can't be certain.'

'Why not?'

'He had a telephone call at his digs from a woman he

can't have known well, if at all. He left the house after telling his landlady that he wouldn't be late back. That was Wednesday and since then there's been no word from him. He was due to phone me to make his usual report, but didn't; he missed his fiancée's birthday.'

'You're assuming that the woman who phoned was something to do with ALFA?'

'Of course.'

'He might have taken off with her and just hasn't had the chance to get in touch with either you or his fiancée.'

'We pay his money into an account in Radlington. He's drawn out every Friday, to see himself through the next week and pay the landlady, but he didn't draw a penny yesterday. If he'd been with a woman all the time, he'd have needed money.'

'Surely he might . . .'

'I can work out all the mights better than you can. I can also see how bloody grim the pattern's become. It's likely he asked the one question too many.'

Because of the pressure King had put on him? wondered Bowles. 'You think they may have murdered him?'

'Or kidnapped him and are now trying to find out how much he knows and has passed on.'

'And the only lead you've left is through Sanderson?'

'Right.'

Bowles stared at the blank television screen. Almost half a minute passed. 'No,' he said finally.

King's voice rose. 'What d'you bloody mean, no?'

'There are just too many suppositions, Mike. He maybe has been exposed because he asked too many questions; maybe someone in ALFA has decided to get rid of him before he can do any real harm; maybe the woman who phoned him was part of ALFA; maybe they've killed him; maybe they're holding him for questioning so that if you could move fast you could still save him . . . What's to say for certain that he hasn't just gone off with a woman for a dirty weekend?'

'He's not drawn a penny. He forgot his fiancée's birthday.'

'If he's off with another woman, he'll hardly want to remember that. The woman might have money so that he doesn't need to dip into his own pocket.'

'Now it's you who's bloody supposing.'

'It's because there's room for me to do so that I'm refusing you the information.'

'You're a real bleeding-heart liberal.'

Bowles tried to joke. 'I count that as one better than the Commie you called me last time!'

'Well, see how your bleeding heart reacts to the news that my lad who's vanished is Reg Newton.'

Bowles guessed the answer before he put the question. 'Bert's son?'

'Yes.'

Albert Newton had been at the training college at the same time as both of them. Whereas he and King had never been more than acquaintances, he and Newton had become the firmest of friends. Newton had been best man at his wedding; he was godfather to Reginald. And after Newton had been fatally injured trying to stop a car, he'd done what he could to help the family. Inevitably, after he'd left the police he'd seen less of them, but they'd always known that they'd only to ask for help and, if possible, he'd give it . . .

'Reg could well still be alive. But it won't be for much longer if we don't find him.'

What had that sergeant lecturer with a beer-belly been so fond of saying? A policeman's duty is to the public and therefore he must never take his personal life to work. Fine words. But the sergeant had never explained how one separated the two when they conflicted.

'They'll be putting every conceivable pressure on him.'

'Isn't that what you're doing to me?' demanded Bowles bitterly.

'All I'm trying to do is to get you to face your real duty.'

Morally, he hadn't any option because Reg's fate couldn't alter the duty he owed; emotionally, he hadn't any option because Reg's fate was infinitely more important than any principle. Right was wrong and wrong was right . . .

'I'll tell you. But only on one condition.' His voice was strained.

'What?'

'That you don't go to his home.'

'Why not?'

'Then there'll be no reason for his family to know anything unless he decides to tell them.'

King's expression was scornful.

'Do you promise you won't do that?'

'D'you want me to go before a bloody justice of the peace to swear it? What are his name and address?'

'I'll have to get back to the Manor to check the address.'

'Then let's move.'

When Bowles returned home, Maggie was watching the television news and she only looked up very briefly as he entered the sitting-room. 'Can you beat it! Parliament's put up their own salaries by twenty-five per cent less than a week after the government said the workers must restrict their pay demands to a maximum of five per cent. How hypocritical can they get?'

He went over to the small cupboard. 'Would you like a drink?'

'Yes, please.' She studied him, far more closely than before. 'You look . . . Is something wrong? John's not in trouble?'

He shook his head. He poured out two whiskies and when he handed her one glass she was surprised by the size and strength of the drink. It was unlike him to turn to alcohol for help. 'Pat, something has happened—what?'

'I've betrayed myself,' he replied, and the pain in his voice prevented his words being theatrically absurd.

She didn't understand what he meant, but she called him to her and tried to comfort him.

CHAPTER 15

The phone rang as Judith was putting a fractious Bob to bed. She shouted out: 'Get it, will you?' Then she turned back to her son, who had a book in his hand. 'Isn't that the one you want her to read to you?'

He considered the question at length. 'I don't know.'

'Then suppose you just . . .' The phone was still ringing. 'Steve!'

'Just going,' he replied from downstairs.

'Bob, hurry up and decide whether you do want this book or, if you don't, which one it is that you do; if not, you'll have to listen to whichever one Mandy chooses.'

'I don't like Mandy.'

'That's being very stupid. She's a charming girl. No more nonsense from you and straight into bed.'

Like any intelligent child, he was a sharp judge of how far he could take things before the pleasure gained from being a nuisance became too expensive. 'I want this book.' He indicated the one in his hand.

'Then since that's settled, into bed with you.'

Once in bed, he said: 'Is he coming back with you?'

'Is who coming back with me from where?'

'Him.'

'You're beginning to annoy me very much. Just who are you talking about?'

'Steven,' he answered reluctantly.

'For goodness' sake, what a ridiculous question. Of course he is.'

'Why?'

'Because it's as much his home as yours and mine.'

'Why?'

'Because each of us loves the other two.'

'I don't. I . . .' He noticed her expression and prudently stopped.

'Steve works very hard to keep you happy and well fed and don't you ever forget that . . . Now I must go and get ready. I'll look in just before we leave and say good night.'

'I wish . . .'

'Well?'

He didn't answer.

As she walked along the narrow passage, she wondered if she'd handled matters well. Probably not, since she'd all but lost her temper. The pundits would not approve. But those who wrote books dealing with questions raised in child care and upbringing had the inestimable advantage of also being able to provide the answers without fear of suffering the consequences of applying them . . .

The bathroom lay between their bedroom and Bob's and before moving in they'd spent more on modernizing and beautifying it than on any other room in the house. Every time she used it, she felt a touch of Ideal Homes class. She laid out fresh clothes, stripped, showered. She half dressed, made up carefully, slipped on a hand-embroidered blouse and a long skirt. She cleaned the full-length mirror of condensation and studied her reflection. It might not be up to her to remark on the fact, but she was looking rather good.

She collected her evening bag from the bedroom and went downstairs. Collins was standing in the centre of the sitting-room, his head only an inch under the main beam.

She waited for him to speak, then asked with a touch of impatience: 'Well, will I do?'

'You look fine.'

'That, I trust, is typical British understatement . . . Mandy not arrived yet?'

'No.'

'Damn!' She looked at her watch. 'I asked her to be here sharp at seven-thirty because the Tibbets always get hot and bothered if one's late.'

He cleared his throat. 'Judith . . .'

'Well?'

'I'll have to drop you at the Tibbets'.'

'Yes, my sweet, I expect you will since we're having dinner with them!'

'You don't quite understand. I'll have to leave you there on your own.'

'You're wrong. I don't understand at all. What on earth are you talking about?'

'The phone call I had earlier on was to say . . . I have to go and see someone tonight.'

'Who?'

'Patrick Bowles.'

'The man who phoned you the other day?'

He nodded.

'Why d'you want to see him tonight when you know you have a dinner date?'

'Because it's terribly important.'

'Exactly what is so terribly important?'

'Please, just accept that something is.'

'I can't. A man phoned and left you so upset that I thought something awful had happened; now he rings again and you say you have to go and see him even though you've a previous engagement and you'll drop me at the Tibbets' and leave me to make all the excuses. You must be able to understand that I have to know why you're behaving so totally out of character.' She saw the stubborn look on his face and her tone became pleading. 'D'you remember what we promised each other the week before we were married? No matter what happened, how annoyed we became with each other, if challenged we'd always speak the absolute truth. Please, I want to hear the absolute truth.'

'Later.'

'No, now.'

'It's impossible until everything's cleared up.'

'Until what is cleared up?'

'I'm sorry. I just can't tell you.'

She became angry, as much because of worry as anything. 'In other words, you don't trust me?'

'It's not a question of trust . . .' He faltered. If and when she learned the truth, she surely would view his past behaviour as a complete breach of trust.

She was about to say something more when the front doorbell rang. Grateful for the interruption, he hurried out of the sitting-room into the hall and opened the front door. Mandy came bouncing in; an eighteen-year-old, overweight, cheerful villager who was happy to babysit at weekends. 'Sorry I'm a bit late, Mr Collins, but Dad suddenly wanted me to get him some supper even though when I asked him half an hour before he said he didn't want any and so I had to cook some eggs and bacon . . .' She spoke in a rush and great detail. By the time Judith had said good night to Bob, Collins had learned all that had happened in the past twenty-four hours in Mandy's home.

They walked in silence round to the garage; a miserable, not companionable silence. She was waiting for him to tell her the truth and he was too scared of the consequences to do so . . .

The short journey was almost equally silent and by the time they reached the Tibbets and their pseudo-Georgian house, they'd exchanged no more than a couple of sentences.

There were three cars parked around the circular turning-circle and as he drew up behind the second Bentley, he tried to break the icy atmosphere. 'I ought to have put up a sticker saying, My Ferrari is being serviced in Modena.'

'Are you still determined to drive off and leave me?'

'Please trust me.'

'You don't make that easy.' She stepped out of the car, slammed the door shut, walked over to the portico and did not look back.

He drove round the turning-circle and back up the drive. He'd once read that man could only be content when he truly believed that the past was finished. Such a man might be content, but he'd also be a fool. The past always survived and threatened both present and future . . .

He hated Bowles for betraying him to King. King was going to demand names. When he'd joined ALFA, he'd had to swear his loyalty in a ceremony which he had found both childish and yet strangely impressive. His oath had promised total and eternal allegiance to the liberation of animals and all who served that cause. When they had discussed the possibility of gaining much greater publicity by carrying out hard jobs, he'd argued against the idea, but had accepted their final decision while making it clear that he would not commit any act of violence. It was because of the oath that, after his arrest, he'd refused to tell the police anything, even though his own companions had called him traitor and threatened him with death . . . After the raid in which a guard had been injured, he had for the first time begun to question whether his allegiance should be total and eternal, but had fudged the issue by assuming that the man had been injured by mistake, since they had panicked. But to kidnap and perhaps kill a detective because he had been trying to infiltrate the organization showed an evil to which there could be no allegiance. So now he would name those names which he could. Except for one. Moira. Love and passion—and could any man, as opposed to every woman, distinguish between the two?—created a unique bond and to betray that was utterly to degrade it. There was that side to Moira's character which had finally frightened and repelled him, but however perverted she might be, he was quite certain that she would never take any part in an action which could lead to murder . . .

The hotel, out in the countryside, had been built fifteen years before the motorway had been projected and the commercial assumption had been that there would always be a very good trade from travellers going to, or returning from, the Continent. After the motorway had been built, few such travellers stayed there and now it looked what it was, run-down, able to make sufficient profit to warrant its remaining open but not enough to cover depreciation, so that when the state of disrepair became too great, it would be closed and the site redeveloped.

He parked outside, went in and saw King, seated at the bar. The years didn't seem to have changed the Detective Chief Superintendent at all—even his pugnacious expression was exactly as he remembered it from the last occasion on which they'd met. He said good evening and the only answer was a grunt. King's glass was full and there was no need to offer him a drink, so he asked the bartender for a gin and tonic. When he'd been served, King said they'd go over to one of the tables; it wasn't a suggestion, but an order.

They sat and since the only other people present were at the far end of the room, there was no fear of their being overheard. 'You know what's been happening?' said King, his voice harsh.

'Patrick's told me, yes.'

'You understand that one of my chaps is missing and

there's every chance he's been kidnapped and is being tortured to give information?'

'Yes.'

'I have to find him bloody fast. If I don't, it may be too late.'

'According to Patrick, it may well be too late already.'

King was annoyed. There was less emotional pressure if the hostage were dead. 'You know the names of the people in the hard cells.'

'The names of those in my cell, yes, but not of others. There was no lateral contact between cells. And you know who were with me, don't you?'

'All right. So what you do now is identify who gave the orders. Someone in each cell has to have a contact to whom he can pass information and from whom he receives orders.'

'As far as I was concerned, it was mostly done by phone.'

'But not always?'

'Occasionally not.'

'Who was your contact?' King then said: 'In fact, you can also give me the name of someone very close to the top, if it's not the same person.'

'No, I can't.'

'That's what one of the other defendants at your trial stated.'

'I can give you one name only and he wasn't near the top.'

'How can you be certain of that?'

'Because he never took decisions, but always had to refer to someone else for them to be made.'

'Then he'll know who makes the decisions?'

'Unless there's another layer of command.'

'What's his name?'

'Colin Maude.'

'Where's he live?'

'In Westley—I can't be more precise than that.'

'Is there anything more you can tell me that'll help?'

'I don't think so. And if that's all, I'd better get back; I'm meant to be at a dinner-party.'

'A social life!' sneered King.

'Only very occasionally.' Collins drained the glass, put it down on the table. 'I hope to God you find him alive.' There was no reply. 'Look, from the beginning I tried to stop them turning to any violence. I said we had to act within the existing framework of the law or we ceased to have right on our side.'

'But you never did anything useful when they started breaking the law, did you? If they'd been stopped then, my lad wouldn't be missing now. Don't you forget that when you're enjoying your dinner-party.'

Collins was shocked by the hatred and contempt in King's voice.

The news was given to King as he waited for the results of the police's visit to Maude's house. A body had been found in an empty house and the dead man's description fitted Reginald Newton; he had been bludgeoned to death. A preliminary medical report placed death as having occurred three days previously.

King cursed violently. Experience could tell a man, but hope could prevent his listening. And, Christ! how he'd hoped . . .

CHAPTER 16

Two police cars converged on the last house in the village of Westley and the crews, led by a detective-inspector, covered all sides of it before the DI knocked on the front

door. Maude was a mild, inoffensive man and his wife
was equally nondescript. When the DI suggested Maude
accompany them back to the central police station so that
he could have a chat with the Detective Chief Superintendent, he was so scared that he didn't try to refuse.

They left a little after eleven and crossed the drive to
the Escort, looking a little forlorn in the company of two
Bentleys and a Porsche.

'Give me the keys,' said Judith.

'I can still say Percival Posslethwaite and not spit,' replied
Collins.

'I'd rather not take the risk of your smacking into Gerald
Ancaster's car, since he's the Deputy Chief Constable.'

He chuckled. 'Do you really prosecute a man with whom
you've drunk wine?'

'In your case, far too much wine. Give me the keys,
please.'

'All right, all right. I'll not rest on my machismo and
insist on driving.'

They settled in the car. The other guests had followed
them out and first one Bentley left, then the other; the
engine of the Porsche fired with the harsh crackle beloved
by every aficionado, but it did not drive away immediately
because Tibbet was talking to the passenger. Judith turned
the ignition key; the engine refused to fire. She tried again
with the same result. 'Shit!' she said violently.

'I didn't realize you knew such language!'

'There seems to be a lot you don't damn well know about
me.' She tried again; the engine fired, then died.

Tibbet stepped back and the Porsche drove off. He turned
and looked at the Escort and although she knew it was
almost certainly imagination, she saw on his face an expression of weary resignation; the poor were always with
one. 'Will you bloody well start, you broken-down wreck!'

The engine fired, faltered, she accelerated hard to send the revs racing, the engine settled down to a steady beat.

'The infallible cure for any recalcitrant piece of machinery,' he said. 'Kick it as you curse it.'

'If only to hell that worked on humans.'

'Steady on, you sound really fierce. Is something wrong? I mean, apart from the car showing its age.'

'If you weren't tight, I'd suggest you asked if anything's right—it would be much quicker for me to answer.'

She drove forward and Tibbet waved them on their way, an expression of relief—or so she saw—on his face. They reached the end of the drive, turned left on to the road, and she accelerated hard. There was a corner almost immediately and she had to break fiercely.

'If you ask me,' he said, 'it's I who should have insisted on driving.'

'I had one glass of white wine, one of red, and no brandy.'

'You could fool me.'

'That's why you thought it would be so easy to fool me, I suppose.'

'You're really in an odd mood.'

'Is that so surprising when I arrive at the Tibbets' and have to apologize for your not being with me and then you turn up in the middle of the meal to cause chaos?'

'That was only because they can't envisage life lived at a lower social level. I said, don't bother with the foie gras, I'll dig straight into the duck in orange. But Angela couldn't imagine anyone eating a meal without a starter and had to tell the staff to feed me the first course while everyone else had to wait and no doubt the cook had hysterics in the kitchen.'

'It would have been better if you'd stayed away.'

'That's a wonderful thing for my wife to say!'

'Then you do remember that I am your wife?'

'For God's sake, either you had a lot more than two glasses of wine or they served you vinegar.'

'You're most amusing.'

'Sure. Only nobody's amused.'

They reached the crossroads which marked their village and, as they turned right and their headlights swept across one wall of the pub at the corner, he said: 'Are you going to explain to my befuddled brain what's going on?'

She did not answer. They passed half a dozen bungalows on their left, a field of wheat on their right, came to their small orchard and immediately past that turned into their drive. In the garage, he climbed out of the car and switched on the overhead light. He'd drunk well, but was far from drunk, yet even so he hadn't the slightest idea what it was had so upset her.

She left the garage without a word, a lighted torch in her right hand. He shut the garage doors, followed her. By the time he stepped into the house, she was talking to Mandy with all her usual cheerfulness and he wondered, not for the first time, how it was that women could so easily and convincingly change faces. Mandy left and Judy went upstairs to Bob's room to make certain he was sleeping soundly. Collins called up: 'Is there anything you want from down here?'

'No.'

He locked and bolted the front door and had reached the foot of the stairs when the telephone rang.

'Steven, it's Patrick Bowles here. I've been trying to get hold of you as I expect your wife's mentioned. I want to say how terribly sorry I am for having to pass on your name and address to Mr King, but the reason . . .'

'You swore it would never happen.' He wished he could order his mind more clearly so that he could say precisely how bitterly furious he was . . .

'There are times, Steven, when unfortunately a man owes two duties which are opposed to each other and so he can only honour one of them. I gave Mike King the information because I accepted that a man's life was at stake and the information might help to save him. I was not to know then that he was dead.'

'You're saying the missing detective's dead?'

'I'm afraid that his body has been found; he was killed on the night he went missing.'

'Then you've no excuse for goddamn betraying me, have you?'

'I'm trying to explain that at the time . . .'

He slammed down the receiver. He went up the stairs, holding on to the banisters, and into their bedroom. Judith was in bed, reading. 'Who was that?' she asked.

He lied without thought. 'A wrong number.'

'It took you rather a long time to discover that.'

'The other chap decided that even if he didn't know me from Adam, he'd like a chat; mostly about Eve.'

'Perhaps he'd also drunk too much.'

'Still bitching hard—why?'

'You've no idea?'

'How could I?'

'By remembering what you told me earlier.'

'What exactly?'

'That you were leaving me at the Tibbets' because you had to see a man called Patrick Bowles.'

'I did.'

'Won't you ever learn that you're not cut out to be any good as a liar? When you don't give yourself away, something else does. Before we started the meal, there was a telephone call for you; naturally, I took it. The caller had twice tried to get hold of you at home and the second time, since it was obviously urgent, Mandy had given him the Tibbets' number. I told him you weren't there and suggested he rang another time.'

'I don't see what all this has to do with your being so bitchy.'

'Did I forget to mention his name? It was Patrick Bowles.'

He desperately tried to clear his mind sufficiently to find some way of extricating himself from the corner into which he'd caged himself. 'You're surely not suggesting it was the same man?'

'Even in this computer age, it's impossible to be in two places at once. What I am saying is, whoever you did see, it certainly wasn't Patrick Bowles.'

Stupidly, he tried to pursue his line of defence. 'There are hundreds of people with that name.'

'You really think I'm naïve enough to believe that coincidentally you were meeting one of them whilst another was telephoning you? . . . Look at me.'

Reluctantly, he faced her.

'Do you promise me that it was another Patrick Bowles whom you saw this evening?'

'I swear it was.'

Her tone became still more bitter. 'I only wish to God I could make myself believe you, but I can't . . . Are you going to tell me what all this is about?' She waited then, with set face, picked up her book and began to read.

'I am not seeing another woman.'

She did not look up.

'That's what you think.'

'You can read my thoughts? How very unfortunate for you.'

Although it was obvious that King was tired, there was no indication in his manner or appearance of his bitter anger. He said to Maude: 'You're a member of ALFA.'

Maude, frightened, stared fixedly at the far wall of the interview room and the framed list of the rights of people being questioned.

Grafton said: 'There's no harm to that, of course: some of my best friends are members . . . You've done a lot of work for ALFA, so they say.'

Maude ran his tongue along his upper lip. 'I used to.'

'But not now?'

'Something happened and they said I couldn't be so active.'

'I suppose that's referring to the time the members of a hard cell in Radlington were arrested, tried, and convicted?'

King said: 'D'you understand why we've asked you to come here at this time of night?'

'I've not done anything . . .'

'It's because we think you can help us. And if you do, that'll help you because then no one's going to suggest you could have had anything to do with all that's been going on recently—malicious damage, arson, aggravated assault, murder.'

'I wouldn't do any of that,' Maude said wildly.

'Exactly what I've been saying to people who've suggested otherwise.'

'Why should anyone think I would?'

'Because you were the contact for Sanderson's hard cell.'

He stared at King, slack-jawed. 'How . . . how d'you know that?'

'We know a lot of things, but you can still help us. So how much more can you tell us.'

Maude made no reply.

'He's remembering his oath of silence,' said Grafton.

'Of course!' King spoke understandingly. 'When you joined ALFA, you promised not to divulge any details of the organization and when you were recruited into the inner group you were made to swear oaths which called for even greater secrecy. But after you were returned to general service—if I can put it like that—the hard cells committed several very serious crimes. You must realize that an innocent citizen has a duty far greater than any which ALFA could impose to help the law whenever a serious crime is committed.'

They waited and showed no signs of tension or impatience; to have done so would have been to reveal that they knew far less than they were suggesting and if he understood this then he would realize that silence was his best policy.

He fiddled with the lobe of his right ear; his gaze flicked backwards and forwards, carefully never meeting either of theirs.

'When Sanderson betrayed the members of his cell, you were lucky he didn't betray you as well, weren't you?'

'I . . . I swear I didn't know . . .'

'You didn't know that they'd become really hard? I'm going to believe you're still telling me the truth. So now tell me who you reported to?'

'Ron,' he answered immediately, never stopping to think that perhaps they'd passed the boundaries of what they did know.

'And his surname?'

'I never heard it.'

'How did you contact him?'

'I telephoned him, mostly.'

'I expect you remember the number?'

'Radlington seven-five-three-two-three.'

'You said you mostly telephoned him—but you occasionally met him?'

'Once or twice.'

'But even so, you never learned his surname?'

'I swear I didn't.'

'We believe you, Colin, don't make any mistake on that score . . . Tell us what else you know about him.'

His evidence proved to be virtually useless. The man was immensely strong in mind as well as body; he was ugly and privately Maude had always thought of him as Quasimodo, even though not a hunchback. But as to his true identity . . .

'He was the top man?'

'I think so.'

'But you can't be certain that he did not, in turn, have to report to someone else?'

He shook his head.

'I've been told Steven Sanderson knew someone near the top. Is that right?'

'So they said.'

'Who was it?'

'The woman he was supposed to be so keen on.'

'What's her name?'

'It's . . . It's not an ordinary one; I mean, one doesn't come across it all that often.'

'Alberta, Claudia, Esmeralda, Minna, Rosanne, Wanda, Zoe?'

'Moira,' he said suddenly.

CHAPTER 17

The message came over the radio as King drove even more furiously than usual and Grafton was silently calling on St Christopher.

'Charlie One, come in please. Romeo Romeo Papa, over.'

Grafton leaned forward and picked up the receiver, trying not to notice the approaching corner as he did so. He pressed the transmit button. 'Hullo Romeo Romeo Papa. Charlie One, over.'

'Charlie One, I have a message for you. The telephone number belongs to a public call-box in Villiers Street, North Radlington.'

'Bugger!' said King, even though he had not really expected the number Maude had given him to provide a strong lead.

Grafton translated that into: 'Message received and understood.'

Collins awoke suddenly and initially all he was conscious of was that his head was pounding and his stomach didn't feel too good either. Then he heard the doorbell ring and this was followed by a hammering on the front door. He looked at the clock, the luminous hands of which said that the time was ten past three. He switched on the bedside light, threw back the bedclothes.

'Who d'you think it can be?' Judith asked nervously.

'God knows!'

'Be careful.'

'If anyone wanted to cause trouble, he wouldn't be hammering on the door.' He climbed out of bed, felt his stomach lurch, went over to the nearer cupboard and brought out of it his dressing-gown.

'Look out of the window and see who it is first,' she suggested.

He should have thought of doing that; if his head had been clearer, he would have done. He went over to the window, which was half open, and leaned out. In the sparse moonlight, he could see two men who stood by the front door, but could identify neither. 'What d'you want?' he called out.

They stepped back and looked up. One of them said: 'Detective Chief Superintendent King and Detective-Constable Grafton. I want to speak to you again.'

'D'you know what the time is?'

'Naturally.'

'Can't it wait?'

'If it could, we wouldn't be here now.'

He said he'd be down to let them in and withdrew his head.

'They say they're detectives. Are you sure that's true,

Steve? They're not pretending to be detectives in order to get into the house?'

'I recognize one of them.'

'What can they want? And why come here in the middle of the night?'

'I'll go and find out; you stay in bed.'

She hesitated, then said in a rush: 'I know I've been on and on at you, but if you're in some sort of trouble, you must tell me so I can help you.'

'I'm not in any sort of trouble.'

'But . . .'

'Almost certainly, all they want is information.'

'About what?'

'About something that happened in the past and isn't any kind of a threat to us now.'

'The man you spoke to just now said he wanted to talk to you again. When did he speak to you before – last night?'

It wasn't the first time that he'd wished she was a little less perspicacious.

'Was it?'

'Yes,' he answered, as he crossed to the door.

'Then you are in trouble!'

'I said, all they want is information. What they refuse to understand is that I can't give it to them.'

He switched on the landing light, went downstairs, unlocked and unbolted the front door. He led King and Grafton into the sitting-room, warning them to duck their heads as they passed under the lintel. The bedroom above was Bob's and despite the fact that sound carried very easily through the thin ceiling, there was no possibility that Judith could overhear their conversation. Once the door was shut, he said: 'I don't know what the law says about waking someone in the middle of the night . . .'

'It's silent and leaves it to the individual police officer's discretion. If the matter is not urgent, he naturally waits until daytime; if it is urgent, he doesn't.' Nor, he could have added, if the underlying intention was to catch the person interviewed at his most vulnerable.

'What is so urgent that you have to wake us up at three in the morning?'

King said contemptuously: 'I suppose you consider your sleep of much greater consequence than another man's life?'

'That isn't the case. Tragically, the man you were looking for is dead.'

'Who says he is?'

'Mr Bowles rang me earlier to try to explain why he'd given you my name and address. He told me that the detective's body has been found and he was killed days ago.'

Thereby, thought King, destroying the sense of extreme urgency which he'd needed to pressure Collins into talking. He silently cursed Bowles for having so active a conscience that he could not live in silence with the consequences of his own decision. 'Yes, he's dead. And now I'm going to find who killed him.'

'I've told you all I can.'

'No, you have not.'

'I gave you Colin Maude's name. He's the only person outside my cell I knew who was in the action group.'

'Back at the time of the trial, one of the other accused said you knew someone who was very close to the top. Maude tells us the same thing.'

'He's either mistaken or lying.'

'Her name is Moira.'

He felt as if he'd received a blow which left him short of wind.

'Who is she?'

'I don't know anyone of that name,' he answered hoarsely.

'Listen. One of my lad's been battered to death. They used clubs to fracture his skull, pulp an eye, shatter his teeth, break his ribs, rupture his intestines, and mash his testicles. He died in the kind of agony you wouldn't even want to read about.

'Both his mother and his fiancée have had to be told. I had to explain to his fiancée that he won't ever be waiting in front of the altar as she walks up the nave. You'll not have had to live with the knowledge that you've pitchforked people into a living hell because you gave the orders which led to a man's death . . .' He stopped, suddenly realizing he was exposing his own emotional agony.

Grafton, to give King time to recover, said: 'They've gone mad, Mr Collins, like we feared and they've got to be stopped. Next time, maybe there won't be one person dead and two persons' lives shattered, there'll be a dozen dead and scores of shattered lives.'

'I've told you as much as I can.'

'Who is Moira?'

'I don't know anyone by that name.'

'Why should Maude lie about her?'

'Probably it's his way of trying to get his own back because I gave you his name.'

King spoke again, his voice hard and bitter. 'My DC's just told you that maybe the next time there'll be a much more tragic incident. I'm saying that it's not maybe, it's for certain. If we don't identify the murderers and whoever's leading them, it's their intention to start a campaign of bombing. Bombers don't care who they rip to pieces; men, women, kids, all come the same to a bomb.'

There was a silence, which Collins broke. 'The woman I knew and whom Maude's probably talking about could never be mixed up in something as beastly as that.'

'Leave us to make certain.'

'No.'

King turned to Grafton. 'We're wasting our bloody time.' He led the way out of the sitting-room, crossed the hall, opened the front door and left.

Collins stood in the doorway, his head thumping and his stomach churning as much from tension as the after-effects of alcohol. He experienced a childish desire to run away and leave the mess for someone else to clear up.

Moments later, he moved. He switched off the sitting-room lights, relocked the front door and pushed home the bolts, went upstairs. Judith was sitting up in bed and she stared at him with an expression he'd never seen before. 'Who's Moira?' she demanded.

He was so shocked that for a while he couldn't think of an answer. He blurted out finally: 'I don't know anyone with that name . . .'

'Still lying,' she said bitterly. 'I was so frightened you were in trouble and wouldn't tell me because you didn't want me to worry, that I had to know what was happening. I went into Bob's room and eavesdropped more thoroughly than last time. Who is Moira? Who's been battered to death? Why are people going to be killed by a bomb? Who's Colin Maude? In God's name, Steve, tell me what's going on. I'm going crazy with worry.'

He slumped down on to a corner of the bed.

'Why won't you answer me, even now?'

'Because I'm terrified.'

'Of what?'

'Of losing you.'

'You don't understand what I mean when I say I love you?' She held out her arms. 'Come here and tell me.'

He did not move.

She dropped her arms. 'You're going to have to explain eventually, so why not now?'

He was silent for a while, then he began to speak disjointedly; he told her all that had happened.

She stared beyond the bed, her eyes unfocused. 'Then when we met, everything you told me about yourself was a lie?'

'At first, I didn't dare tell you the truth in case you'd

have nothing more to do with me. Afterwards, it was too late.'

'Why?'

'Because I'd have shown myself to be a liar.'

'A liar for a short while, yes. But did you have so little faith in me that you couldn't believe I'd understand and honour you for having the strength of character to face me and speak the truth as soon as that became necessary? As it is, you've been living a lie ever since we met. It's only now I can understand things such as why you wouldn't drive to Wem.'

'I just thought . . .' He stopped.

'That my love was fair-weather only?'

'I'd trapped myself. The longer I left any explanation, the more impossible it became to make it.'

She turned and stared at him with sharply focused gaze. 'Who is Moira?'

'You heard me tell them . . .'

'They probably didn't believe you any more than I do. Who is she?'

'A woman I knew.'

'When?'

'While I was with ALFA. We parted before the trial.'

'Then there's only one more thing I want to know about her. You say you parted before the trial, but have you been seeing her since we've been married?'

'Of course I haven't.'

'Of course? It's strange. Until tonight I'd have said that I could name any number of "of courses" about you, now I discover that there aren't any. Last night I went to bed with one man, now I find I'm with another. I suppose that could make me some sort of whore.'

'Stop talking like that.'

'Would you rather I played your game and pretended that nothing's happened?'

'I've tried to explain . . .'

'Yes, Steve. And I've tried to understand. But I can't. I simply cannot understand how if you loved me as much as I've loved you, you could make our marriage one long lie.'

'But I couldn't tell you at the beginning that I was a convicted criminal . . .'

'I'm too bewildered to go on any more. Leave it and we'll give ourselves time to think.' She switched off her bedside light, moved down in the bed, and turned so that her back faced him.

He stood, removed the dressing-gown and returned it to the cupboard. Because he was something of a fool, he had not understood how even more deeply she would be hurt if he did not voluntarily tell her the truth . . .

King said bitterly: 'He'd have told us who she was if that bloody fool hadn't phoned him and said Reg was dead.' They were on dual carriageway and the speedometer was showing ninety-five. Grafton briefly wondered why there was never a policeman around when you needed one—in this case to flag them down for speeding.

'She could lead us straight to the top.'

That wasn't certain. But the Detective Chief Superintendent was a man who not only demanded complete loyalty, he also gave it, and from the moment he'd learned that Newton was missing, he had ceased to be his usual sharp, logical self. 'What about getting back on to Maude?'

'He's told us all he can.'

'Then we're stuck. It seems likely Collins knew a woman called Moira who possibly could name the person who's running the hard group, but he's not admitting anything and we can't prove he's lying; even if we could prove that, we've no way of forcing him to tell the truth.'

'You give in bloody easily.'

'Only when I have to, Guv. We've nothing more to go

on than a vague rumour which was going around at the time of the trial and Maude's statement. Where can anyone go from there?'

'Depends if he's got brains and balls.'

'I've never had any complaints about the latter.'

'So try thinking as well.'

They passed a thirty sign at something over seventy. Then the road became lined by houses and was met by other roads and finally King reduced speed. 'Well?'

'Thinking can't alter the facts.'

'Then remember this one all-important fact. At the trial, they believed Sanderson had shopped them and they threatened to kill him.'

'Only because that's the line you fed 'em in order to persuade them to talk and . . . Christ! You're not thinking of slipping them his present name and address?'

'Why not?'

'I can think of half a dozen reasons, the most immediate of which is that they might decide to try to carry out their threat.'

'Are you forgetting that Reg has been murdered?'

'I'm forgetting nothing. I'll work twenty-five hours a day to discover who the bastards were and to send them down for their lifetimes. But I'm not ready to do that over Sanderson's corpse.'

'You're not thinking.'

'If you ask me, Guv . . .'

'I didn't.' They passed a World War I tank that commemorated the fallen, a row of small shops, and turned a very sharp corner to enter a much wider road along which were large Victorian houses that had been turned into private and council offices. 'If they learn where Sanderson is living, it's odds on they'll send in a team to get him. We'll be waiting for that team.'

'All right, we're waiting. But things can go wrong and they

could get through and kill him before we can stop them.'

'Only if someone makes a right balls-up.'

'You know Sod's Law. If something can go wrong, it will. If they killed him and it came out that you'd been using him as bait, you'd be hanged, drawn, and quartered.'

'It's a risk I have to take.'

'Not with my backing. And I'll speak here and now for everyone else—it'll be without their backing as well.'

'Scared?'

'Sufficiently scared, yes, not only on my own behalf, but also on yours as well.'

They passed the fire station, one of whose wide doors was open so that the pump appliance could drive out immediately.

King spoke quietly, without any of the emotion shown previously. 'Suppose I tell you that I have no option?'

'Then I'd answer that it's time you started thinking factually and not emotionally.'

'You're bloody impertinent.'

'Yes, Guv. When I reckon I need to be.'

They came up to lights, set at red, and stopped. A lorry, its exhaust note throbbing and echoing from the plate glass windows of shops, turned right and came past them.

'I have no option,' said King. 'I can't give you the details, but there's every reason to believe that a job is being planned which has to be prevented, no matter at what cost.'

'All right, I'll accept that. But what happens if you take the risk and something does go wrong—is anyone going to cover you from the fall-out or will it be a case of politics and you'll be abandoned and left to carry the shit?'

'Left to carry it,' replied King as the lights changed and he drove forward. 'The man who actually breaks the rules always is.'

'Then forget the idea.'

'I cannot.'

CHAPTER 18

Collins levered the fork back to bring up a clod of earth; he tried to break up the clod with the tines, but it was like hitting a rubber ball. He wiped the sweat from his forehead with the back of his hand.

Bob appeared in the doorway of the kitchen. 'Lunch,' he called out.

'Thanks very much. Never has a call to leave a mess to go to a mess been more welcome.' Bob stared blankly at him, then returned inside. Was he ever going to break through that dislike and regain the friendly companionship they'd first known? How long could he reasonably be expected to go on knocking his head against the brick wall of Bob's antagonistic behaviour? Wasn't he entitled . . . He cut short his thoughts, recognizing that they were a cover for his own bitterness at the way Judith was behaving. He'd slept after the two detectives had left. When he'd woken up, he'd found that her half of the bed was empty. Downstairs, she'd said that she'd been unable to sleep so had got up, obviously without waking him since he'd gone on snoring. The inference had been obvious. Only a man without feeling could have slept and snored . . . He'd tried to explain things again. He'd been met by a dispassionate, unshakable refusal to understand which had left him floundering. Later, Bob, with the brutal instinct of the young, had divined that they were at loggerheads, even though they were not openly arguing, and had done his best to exacerbate the situation . . .

He put the fork in the garden shed, changed his shoes, crossed the corner of the lawn and the gravel path to the kitchen. It was their habit on Sundays to enjoy a pre-lunch drink. 'What will you have? Sherry, vermouth, or there may still be some Dubonnet left?'

'I don't want anything,' she answered.

'It's Sunday. We always have a drink now.'

'I rather gathered you'd decided to dispense with all traditions.'

'Look, I . . .'

'Can you move, please? I'm a little behind and I know that you like your meal sharp at one.' She spoke with studied patience. She waited until he'd moved and then opened the refrigerator to bring out a pack of margarine. 'You do like the potatoes mashed, don't you? They're better for you, even with a little margarine, than fried or baked. There was a discussion yesterday morning on the correlation between fried foods and heart problems and it seems that statistically there's . . .'

'Does it matter?'

'It certainly does to someone who's in the high risk area. Although, of course, you hold that a person's entitled to behave exactly as he wants, without any reference to how his actions will affect other people.'

'When I was in ALFA, I didn't know you and so you couldn't be affected. It was only afterwards . . .'

'You don't think I was speaking personally, do you?'

'Just as personally as you could get. Judith, we've got to get things sorted out.'

'Yes, dear, if you say so, but not right now, when I'm trying to get the lunch on the table at the precise time you want. If you've nothing better to do, why not go and pour yourself a drink?'

The brick wall was still higher. If only she had attacked him, he could have fought back; but he couldn't fight her air of sweet reasonableness without making himself a complete fool.

He left the kitchen and went through to the dining-room, opened the cupboard, and poured himself a strong whisky.

King replaced the receiver, pushed his chair back until he could stand, walked round the desk to the window and looked out and across the road at the council car park, the church which was partially obscured by several luxuriant horse-chestnut trees, and the vicarage which with its well-kept lawn and garden, its faint air of croquet and cucumber sandwiches seemed out of place in a world in which violence had come to play so large a part.

So far, he had done nothing that could not be undone; the next move, if he took it, would be irreversible. He remembered Patrick Bowles's argument to the effect that the worth of a man's life could not be judged by the consequences of his death. Typical liberal nonsense, seeking equality in death as well as life when there could be equality in neither . . . He reached a decision, certain that consequences were all-important. He pressed down a switch on the intercom and asked DC Benson to come through to his office.

Benson would soon be far too close to middle age to laugh at it and already his forehead was growing as his hair receded; his face was unremarkable and unmemorable; his figure betrayed a love of rich food and there was not much elasticity left in his stride. Most observers would have described him as tired, intent merely on working out his time to a pension. In truth, he was keen, efficient and, if not clever, possessed of a fund of common sense. King would never have kept a man working for him who was not good at the job.

'Brian,' said King, as Benson sat, 'I want you to go up to Radlington and look up the people on this list.' He pushed across a single sheet of paper. Benson half rose to take it. 'They were members of a hard cell in ALFA, convicted on charges of breaking and entering and arson, and jailed. Find out who's likely to be the most receptive and feed him or her the name and address at the bottom. They knew Collins as Sanderson and they believe he shopped them. The moment you've passed it on, let me know; whatever you do, whatever happens, make certain I know immediately.'

'Got it.' Benson carefully folded up the sheet of paper and put it in the breast pocket of his sports jacket.

'That's the lot. Except that your expenses will be scale one. I've passed on word to that effect.'

He stood.

'Remember. Get on to me right away.'

As he left the room, Benson thought that it was totally out of character for the Detective Chief Superintendent to be so keyed-up as to repeat an order he had already given. So just how important must this job be?

King stared at the closed door. Time could dull any emotion. So it was possible that when they learned the new identity of Sanderson, they'd content themselves with obscene letters or telephone calls. But he judged them, and more particularly the people behind them, to have the kind of mean, warped, maladjusted characters that would not be content until brutal revenge had been gained.

Benson was a man seldom remembered; he could merge into a crowd of three, he could chat half the night without saying anything of the slightest consequence. But because he had developed to a fine art the ability of appearing to be flattered by another's attention, he had no difficulty in striking up an acquaintance.

He parked outside the central police station in Radlington and walked up the sloping ramp to the first floor of the concrete and glass building. At the front desk he asked to speak to the detective-inspector. The DI passed him on to the detective-sergeant, who passed him on to one of the duty DCs.

The DC suggested he first of all arranged where he was

to stay and strongly recommended digs in preference to the police hostel, where the food was notoriously bad even by hostel standards; the DC spoke to a prospective landlady over the phone. He then led the way down to the computer room. He settled in front of one of the VDUs, fed in a program and tapped in the names Benson had given him, asked for the details of the first one.

Information came on screen and Benson moved until he could read it without the interference of a reflection from the window. Charles John Halliwell. Last known address, 17, Sweetwater Road, South Radlington. One conviction. General file, H 16984; Photographs, PG 44653; Fingerprints, P 55354; full details of conviction, CT 678734.

'Before we became computerized,' said the DC, 'all the information was on a couple of pages of paper and you could read it as quick as you liked. Now you have to search through a whole ruddy electronic library.'

'That's life,' said Benson unsympathetically. 'What I'm after is trying to work out which of 'em will be the best bet to make contact with.'

'Then you need a run-down on the general files.' The DC entered new commands and up came a list of public houses in the division. He swore.

Collins reached across to the front passenger seat, picked up the briefcase, left the car, walked out of the garage. The bright sunshine made him momentarily screw up his eyelids. It had been fine all day, with hardly a cloud in the sky and earlier in the afternoon the temperature had reached nearly eighty; the English countryside was at its peerless best which made it all the more ironic that in his mood he would have welcomed heavy rain and sodden fields. His rate of walking slowed as he approached the garden gate. How was he going to be received this evening? With the same iceberg politeness as on the previous ones?

The lawn again needed cutting. At least he had a valid excuse for not cutting it tonight. A couple of swallows performed aerial acrobatics, and as he watched them he envied them a life in which the past didn't exist and the future couldn't be comprehended. Then it occurred to him that since swallows returned to the same nesting-site year after year, they must remember something and look forward to something. Perhaps every living thing had a past and a future. A multitude of unhappinesses . . .

As he entered the house, Judith looked out of the kitchen. 'Hullo.'

Was she going to come and kiss him . . . Seconds passed and it was obvious she was not. Another evening of desperately searching for neutral subjects to talk about; subjects which wouldn't suddenly, inexplicably, lead them back to the past. He said: 'I've some work to do, so I'll go straight on up.'

'Have you much?'

'Only an hour or so.'

'Would you rather finish it before we start supper?'

'If that doesn't upset arrangements?'

'I can easily work things so that nothing spoils.'

He crossed to the stairs. From the sitting-room came the sounds of television. According to an article he'd read that morning, the latest research showed that more than three hours of television a day were harmful to younger children. It would be even more harmful to at least one adult to try to restrict Bob's viewing . . .

When he had work to do at home, he used the spare bedroom, where an old kitchen table made a reasonable substitute for a desk. He put the briefcase down on the table, sat, brought out the papers. Dermot Cartright wanted to know whether it would be a good idea to buy a garage on the far side of Oakley Cross and it was his job to check through the garage's accounts for the past three years and identify what fiddles were going on. Cartright always worked on the assumption that everyone was on the fiddle and this had made him a wealthy man. In ten or fifteen years' time he would probably have moved up to the City, buying and selling in millions or tens of millions and never realizing that his actions affected people . . .

He heard Judith approach. She came to a stop just inside the doorway. 'I thought that when you came in you were looking very tired?'

He wondered whether it was wishful hoping to hear concern in her voice. 'It's been a bit of a heavy day with boss-man at his most demanding.'

'Then why not leave that and come down and have a drink?'

'He wants all the answers by nine in the morning.'

'He makes you do far too much.'

'He's a workaholic and can't understand that other people aren't. It would take a much braver or cleverer man than I to bring such fact to his notice.'

'Then I suppose I'd better leave you to get on with things.'

'Unfortunately.'

'D'you really mean that?' She came forward to stand by the chair and rested a hand on his shoulder. 'Even though I've been so beastly?'

'If right now is being beastly, do your demoniac worst.'

She began to stroke his neck with her thumb. 'Steve, I can't stand going on as we have been.'

'And no more can I.'

'But it hurt so much to learn the truth. If only . . . Damn! I swore to myself not to come up here and use those two horrible words.'

'If only I'd told you everything the moment I realized I'd fallen in love with you? I should have done, of course. I can see that now. My father had an old saying: if I'd as much foresight as I've hindsight, I'd be a dealsight the wiser. At

the time, I was so terrified of losing you that I was not only
a coward, but also too thick to understand that you'd accept
that although I'd been branded a criminal, morally I wasn't
one.'

'That was the only reason?'

'What other could there be? I wasn't ashamed of the
truth, just frightened of it. I'd done all I could to stop the
others becoming involved in violence because I just don't
believe such action's ever justified when there are still legal
channels available.'

'Then how could you have been accused?'

'The others believed I'd betrayed them to the police and
in retaliation they all swore I'd worked with them all the
time. I could prove I hadn't taken part in the fire-bomb
raid, but not that I hadn't been on others, or that I hadn't
helped in the planning.'

'But if you were innocent, how could you have been
convicted?'

'I learned the hard way that innocence sometimes isn't
enough.'

'Oh God, it must have been awful for you!'

'Not as bad as it might have been. I only collected a
suspended sentence because the court accepted I'd not been
on that last raid and the police said I'd helped them.'

'Nevertheless, your whole life was wrenched out of shape.'

'I suppose so. But it meant that I met you.' He reached
up to hold her hand.

She gripped him tightly. 'I've been horrible to you for the
past few days.'

'With reason.'

'Stop being magnanimous, it only makes me feel worse.'

'You'd rather I curse you for a heartless bitch?'

'Just this once, maybe.'

He used his free hand to guide her round to sit on his lap.
They kissed with a passion they had not known for days.

'I'd better go,' she said.

'Why?'

'Because you've work to do.'

'And like any well-bred Englishman, I'm expected to put duty before pleasure and gain self-esteem from my masochism?'

'You're talking nonsense.' She kissed him again. 'I love you when you talk nonsense.'

'I know something I can do that makes me even more lovable.'

'Just for the moment, you stick to being a masochist.' She slipped off his lap and stood. 'It's all over, isn't it?'

'There'll be no more ghosts from the past to scare us.'

'Thank God for that.'

After she'd left, he stared through the window. It was a lovely, sunny evening and the countryside looked wonderful.

Benson dialled the number and was answered almost immediately. 'It's Brian, Guv.'

'Well?' said King.

'It's taken a bit of time because I reckoned I daren't rush things, but I've finally managed it. I made contact with one of the blokes—the only woman looked a real battle-axe—and we've been pubbing. He's so mixed-up it's like talking to a red millionaire, but he's clear on one thing: he wants Sanderson's guts for garters.'

'He's no suspicions?'

'Swallowed everything whole and damn near choked on it.'

'Then you can return here right away.'

As Benson left the call-box, he realized that he should have known better than to expect even the briefest 'Well done'.

CHAPTER 19

King looked down at the large-scale map spread out on his desk. Sod's Law. If something could go wrong, it would. Since he had deliberately placed a man's life at risk, he had to make quite certain that nothing could go wrong.

The men who would be setting out to murder Collins were amateurs, but not without experience. They might make their move in daylight, but it would seem much more natural to them to wait until darkness. So a good watch had to be kept during daylight and an even better one at night.

To do a good job, they would need to learn something about their target and that would mean asking questions; but amateurs sometimes went ahead without worrying about details. So while inquiries concerning Collins would suggest they were getting ready to attack, the lack of any such evidence could not be taken as an indication that they had not started to move.

They might decide to act directly or indirectly. Approach the house, cut the telephone wires, break in; this would expose them to the wife and perhaps the stepson, but they'd be wearing ski-masks, or something similar, and they might well know that in moments of high mental stress, memory frequently failed. Or they might break into the garage and plant a bomb in the car, activated either by the ignition or movement. Or they might even, since they were amateurs, decide to act illogically and attack him at his office . . . All the possibilities had to be covered, which meant a large team, so the local force would have to be called on for help; this meant he must square things first with the Assistant Chief Constable so that the divisional superintendent couldn't try to be obstructive . . .

He concentrated on the details of the map. In one respect Brecks Cottage was a difficult place over which to keep watch, in another it was easy. It stood in the middle of fields and therefore could be approached from any angle, but open fields could be covered by movement sensors, borrowed from the army. Direct observation on the drive, garage and house, could be maintained by observers, using image-intensified glasses at night-time.

If he were determined to murder Collins, where and how would he go about it? Not at the office, not in the car, but in the cottage. At night. And the approach? To the south was a four-acre field, a very small stream, and then woods. A vehicle could easily be hidden in the woods, one could cross the stream and approach the house without the slightest risk of being seen from the road. Then that was the obvious route. A clever planner identified the obvious route and chose another. A very clever planner who granted his opponent a good level of intelligence might decide on the 'double take'— because he'd be expected not to take the obvious route, he'd take it. Which, of course, brought one back to the starting point. But if all routes were covered by sensors, all possibilities were taken care of . . . They would probably try to cut the telephone wires. It was unlikely they'd have raised their house-breaking skills to the point where they could gain entry without making a noise, nevertheless the assumption must be made that they had; so ultra-sensitive microphones must be deployed within the arc of the movement sensors . . . He used a soft-leaded pencil to mark in the points at which sensors and microphones should be placed.

He stood upright and pressed a clenched fist into the small of his back which often ached when he maintained any one position, standing or sitting, for long. Since something could always go wrong, identify the weakest link. That had to be Collins. If unsuspecting, he might be lured into a trap. A phone call to the office asking for a meeting in the countryside on a pretext that wouldn't strike him as odd or, if it did, intrigued him sufficiently for him to pursue it. It was obvious how to eliminate this week link—inform Collins of the risk that existed. But do so and Collins might realize that he had been made the bait in a trap . . .

King swore. He couldn't avoid the certainty that he was going to have to warn Collins.

King stood in the sitting-room of Brecks Cottage, well clear of the central beam.

Judith said, her voice strained: 'But how could they have learned Steve's new name and address?'

'We don't know for certain that anyone has, Mrs Collins. I must make that clear. All I'm saying is that we've reason to believe it's possible.'

'It could only have happened if Mr Bowles had passed on the information,' said Collins. 'He'd never have done that.'

'That's right, he wouldn't. But one has to remember that there's always the one chance in a million that someone who knew you before has recently recognized you and passed on the fact.'

'Oh God!' said Judith. 'And we thought it was finally all behind us.'

'It may well be. Please remember what I've said twice—there's no certainty. The only reason I'm here now is because there are one or two elementary precautions that it would be a good idea for your husband to take and which will make it certain that whatever the facts, nothing will happen to him.'

'I'm surprised at your concern,' said Collins.

'That's unfair.' King managed to sound hurt. 'We shall, of course, be keeping a close eye on this house. Even so, keep ground-floor windows shut and catches fast and outside doors locked and bolted at all times. If anyone calls whom you don't recognize, don't let him in, no matter what reasons for entry are given, and this applies twice as strongly after dark. If you have the slightest reason for suspicion, telephone the number I'll give you and help will be with you immediately. Should you try the telephone but find the line's not working, activate the alarm which I will be giving you.'

Judith said: 'According to what you said earlier, there's very little risk; but judging by all these precautions, you think it's a lot more serious than that.'

'Not so. I'm afraid that we're living in times of a high crime rate and the precautions I've suggested are very little more than those any householder should observe. But now I am going to suggest one thing more. Mr Collins, it's always an idea to imagine the worst and work out how to counter that. So let's do this. They've learned of your whereabouts and are determined to carry out their threat. They've examined the problem and have decided the easiest way is to lure you to somewhere isolated and to kill you there. So one of them will telephone you and suggest, for a reason you'd normally find perfectly feasible, that you meet at a designated spot . . . Go nowhere to meet anyone unless you can be absolutely certain that the caller is genuine; even then, go nowhere at all isolated.'

'You were not telling the truth,' said Judith.

'I'm sorry?'

'You don't give that sort of advice to the ordinary prudent householder.'

'I did say I was adding one thing, Mrs Collins. But I'm adding it solely because the threat was made against your husband, not because I believe there's any greater risk.'

'Don't you?'

'I do not.'

Through the sitting-room window, Judith watched the Detective Chief Superintendent climb into his car and drive away. 'He was lying.'

'I don't think so,' said Collins.

'The police haven't just caught a whisper, they've heard something very definite. Someone has identified you.'

'Even if that has actually happened, nothing will come of it. It's a thousand times easier to talk than to do.'

'What about all the terrible things they've already done?' He put his arm around her. 'There's no need to worry . . .'

'There damn well is.'

'If King was telling the truth, then there's virtually no chance of anything happening. Even if he was lying, he's promised the police will protect us. I'm not going to rush off to meet someone I don't know in the middle of Park Wood. So there's no way those maniacs can get at me.'

She looked across at the battery-operated alarm which King had left them. Logically, Steve was right. And yet there was ice inside her . . .

Grafton entered the room in Oakley Cross central police station which King—much to the previous occupier's annoyance—was using as a command centre. 'I think we're on to something, Guv.'

King, who'd been studying the large-scale map for the umpteenth time, looked up.

'I had a drink and a couple of sandwiches at the Cock and Bull . . . Quite a story, eh?'

'What's that?'

'Sorry, just a quick funny. Anyway, I chatted up a neat little number in barmaids and she mentioned that earlier on there'd been someone looking for an old friend with whom he'd lost contact over the years, name of Steven Collins.'

'They're moving!'

'I tried to get a description, of course, but it was useless. Not all that young, but then not all that old; hair was dark brown, or was it light brown?; a kind of a round face . . . You know the way it goes.'

'Accent?'

'A touch of something, but she couldn't identify what; might have been Cornish, Yorkshire, Brummagen . . . If she'd remembered Welsh, she'd have included that.'

'Car?'

'No one saw it.'

'Any reference to area?'

'Not a word as to where he'd come from or was staying.'

'Is there anything to be gained by questioning her officially?'

'You won't learn any more and that'll make her gossip her head off.'

'What did she tell him?'

'That she didn't know any Steven Collins.'

'Are they still trying to trace him? Or have they done that and they now want to know about his lifestyle?'

'If they've an ounce of initiative, it'll be his lifestyle by now.'

'So they're probably well into the planning stage . . . I want another bloke with night glasses watching the house.'

'There'll be two tonight as it is.'

'There'll be three. And another car standing by, fully manned.'

'It's getting like an SAS operation!'

'It had bloody well better move as smoothly.' He looked down at the map yet again. What had he overlooked?

Moira Durack could wear a lightweight sloppy sweater and jeans and yet look smart. Her beauty was striking because it was unusual, a shade ethereal, and possessed depth; her figure was a series of slim, graceful curves; her smile would make a man think of long nights and her low, musical voice could promise even when recounting the alphabet. In her company, few men paused long enough to become even half aware of some strange corner to her character, even fewer tried to analyse what might be concealed within that corner.

She listened to the four men discussing, arguing, repeating themselves, and said nothing until one of the four turned away from the nearer bed, on which a map had been spread out, and went over to the chest of drawers to pour himself a drink. 'No,' she said. She lit a cigarette.

Ronald Prescott added a splash of water to the whisky. A short man, he had such wide, square shoulders that in certain postures he could appear mis-shapen; his face was strikingly ugly.

'You don't cross the field to the house,' she said.

He drank. 'Why not?'

'Because I've a much better idea. We lure him away from the house and kill him somewhere else.'

'We've decided against that.'

'Not against my making the telephone call and my persuading him along for a chat.'

'A chat?' said one of the other three and laughed coarsely.

Prescott said: 'It's been a long time.'

'He won't have forgotten.'

He returned to the nearer bed and stared down at the map. He spoke slowly. 'We've no idea how well the house is protected, have we? Maybe he's been running so scared it's wired up to half a dozen alarms.'

'So we cut the electricity . . .' began one of the others.

'Any decent alarm system has a reserve supply.'

'It'll be one against four—he's not Superman.'

'But he lives in the country and could well own a twelve-bore. D'you feel like looking up the barrels?'

'He wouldn't have a gun, seein' he was a member of ALFA.'

'Not for shooting birds, for shooting people.' Prescott's sense of humour was heavy and none of the other three men smiled. 'We'll think on it.'

They each had another drink and then the three left,

uneasy because they were nervously eager to get the job over
and done with and now it seemed that even the planning was
not yet settled.

Prescott poured out drinks for Moira and himself. He
crossed the floor to the nearer bed and sat on the corner of
it, careful to avoid the map. 'What are you after?'

She answered casually: 'Just trying to make certain things
work smoothly.'

'There's far more to it than that.' He drank. 'You want
to humiliate him first.'

'That's being ridiculous.'

'He kicked you out of his bed and you've never forgiven
him.'

'What I've never forgiven is his becoming a traitor.'

He looked up. 'And the fact that he didn't betray you
along with the others made it even more bitter because it
meant he was patronizing you because he was sorry for
you.'

'You've got marbles loose in your head,' she said angrily.

'It's no good. I know you too well.'

'You think you're so clever when it comes to people . . .
All right, if you are that smart, tell me what's going to
happen when we do meet?'

'First, you'll seduce him.'

'A man I hate?'

'Because you hate him. He's married and so if you make
him betray his marriage, you'll get more pleasure than any
orgasm could ever give you.'

'All right, you're smart. So maybe you realize there are
things about you I don't like?'

'My face for one?'

'The softness behind your face.'

He finished his drink. Perhaps, compared to her, he was
soft; for him, just the death of Steven Sanderson would be
revenge enough.

She came across until she could press against him. She spoke sweetly. 'Is there something about me you don't like?'

His hand seemed to move of its own accord and it began to caress her warm flesh.

'We'll do it my way,' she said softly.

CHAPTER 20

They said that patience was a virtue. In that case, Collins thought, he was not a very virtuous man. 'I've told you already, Mummy's had to go out.'

'Why?' demanded Bob aggressively.

'Because she's on a committee.'

'What's a committee?'

He realized that he'd pointed the way to complicated waters. 'It's a group of people who disagree about everything . . . Now, what do you want for supper? There are fish fingers or those beefburgers which you like so much.'

'I don't want them.'

'You must eat something.'

'Not until Mummy comes home and cooks it.'

'Beefburgers won't taste any different because I put them under the grill instead of her.'

'They're much nicer when she cooks them.'

'I'll guarantee you can't tell the difference.'

'You can't cook.'

'I am an acknowledged expert at boiling an egg. Now, which is it to be—fish fingers or beefburgers?'

'Nothing.'

They said that counting up to ten was a sovereign way of overcoming one's angry impatience; right now, even a hundred wouldn't do the job. 'This, young man, is the last call for dinner. Which would you prefer?'

'I don't want anything.'

'Then it's bath and bed.'

'Not until Mummy's here.'

'You are going to be tucked up in bed and fast asleep when she returns. I am going upstairs now to run the bath and when I call, come on up.'

'I won't.'

'Then you will learn that the back of an old-fashioned hairbrush stings the bottom.'

He went up to the bathroom and began to run the bath. Some international court of justice had ruled that corporal punishment was humiliating, barbarous and therefore illegal—the framers of that particular piece of nonsense had obviously never had children . . . The phone rang and he turned off the tap and went over to the door. He heard Bob lift the receiver; a strange reversal from the previous week when he'd flatly stated that he wouldn't ever answer the phone because it frightened him.

'Is that you, Mummy? Why won't you come home? I'm hungry . . .' He listened, put the receiver down.

'Who is it?' Collins called out.

The only answer was the slammed door of the sitting-room.

He went downstairs and along to the phone.

'Was that your son I was talking to?' a woman asked.

He tried to fit the voice to one of their friends and failed. 'That's right.'

'He sounds charming.'

It was just possible that other people's children could be charming.

'How old is he?'

It seemed a strange question since their friends presumably had a rough idea of how old Bob was. 'He's turned six.'

'Then he's not your son.'

'Who's that speaking?'

'You mean, you don't recognize my voice?'

'I'm afraid not.'

'And all these years I've been consoling myself with the thought that you could never ever forget me!'

A frightening possibility occurred to him. 'Who are you?'

'Guess.'

He said nothing.

'You don't like playing guessing games? Never mind, I'll make it easy for you. I'm someone whom you once knew very well indeed.'

He turned to make certain the sitting-room door was shut before he remembered that Judith was out. 'Moira?'

'So you haven't forgotten me after all!'

'How did you find me?'

'It's very much more important to ask why.'

'Why?'

'To tell you I've managed to save you.'

'Save me from what?'

'The others. If ever they learn your new name and address, they won't ring to give you the news.'

Judith had been right; the danger had been and was much greater than King had been prepared to admit. 'How can you be so certain they don't know?'

'Because all they've learned is that you're living somewhere in the South.'

'You've found out more than that.'

'I was with Joe, the man who was trying to sell them the information just before he was killed in a car accident.'

'He didn't tell them?'

'They weren't yet ready to pay him the price he was asking, so they told me to persuade him . . . At first, Steve, I was going to tell them everything I'd learned.'

'Why?'

'When you walked out of my life, I hated you so much

I'd have done anything to get my own back. But after Joe died in the accident, I stopped to think about things and I realized that if I told them what I now know, they'd kill you, your wife and your child.'

'They'd harm them?'

'Don't you understand anything? They'd do whatever hurt you the most. They'd rape your wife in front of your eyes and then murder her as slowly as they could.'

'Oh Christ!' he mumbled.

'I began to remember the good times, not the bad ones, and suddenly I realized I couldn't tell them anything . . . Steve, you did truly love me, didn't you?'

'What are you going to do?'

'Promise me that you did.'

'Are you certain that all they know is that I live in the South?'

'Steve, I must see you.'

'Why?'

'I know you're married and have a family and your wife wouldn't be best pleased if she learned you were seeing an old girlfriend, but I'm sure you can slip away for just a few minutes.'

'No, I can't.'

'It's no good trying to tell me you're hen-pecked. One of the things which first attracted me was your strength; the certainty that if you wanted to do something, you would. So that means, doesn't it, that what you're really saying is that you don't want to see me.'

'It's so difficult . . .'

'I promise not to make a scene and embarrass you. All I want is for you to look at me and say that you really did love me then. Maybe you don't understand very much about the way women think? Ever since we parted, I've been wondering if you'd really meant all the wonderful things you said, or whether they were just to get me into bed. You see, if you meant them, then it was a love-affair that didn't work out and I can be nostalgic about everything if you didn't, it was just sordid.'

'It was never sordid,' he lied.

'Tell me that face to face. It's so easy to lie over the phone and I must be certain.'

'I don't think I can see you . . .'

'I've taken a terrible risk in coming down here; if they ever find out, they'll kill me. You're not . . . not telling me I've been a fool to do it?'

'I'm very, very grateful, but . . .'

Her voice became shrill. 'Then I have been a fool! If you won't see me, it's because you know I'd realize you didn't mean anything. For you, I was only a bit of fun. And all I'm left with are sordid memories. I shouldn't have bothered to risk my life by coming here.'

He remembered all too clearly how her perversity of character could take many forms. If he persisted in refusing to meet her, she was quite capable of giving them his present name and address. He pictured them, breaking into the cottage, silently making their way up the stairs and into the main bedroom, ripping back the bedclothes, gripping Judith and spreadeagling her legs . . . He said hoarsely: 'I can't come until my wife returns from a meeting.'

'I'll be waiting. Cabin seven, Orchardgreen Motel. And now I know I was right not to tell them.'

Judith drove past the garage and up as close to the garden gate as she could go, left the engine and headlights on as she waited for Collins to come out to meet her. In the face of King's warnings, they had determined to live as normal a life as possible while taking all precautions. Unknown to her, three men on the raised ground beyond the road watched with approval as the outside house lights were switched on and Collins, a stout stick in his right hand, came round the side of the house. He opened the gate, waited for her to switch off the car lights and engine, and unlock the driving door and climb out, then together they went round to the front door.

'Has anything happened?' she asked as they approached the door.

'Nothing much.'

There was sufficient light coming through the window on their right for her to see his face. 'What exactly does "nothing much" mean?'

'Nothing to cause a panic. King phoned earlier.'

She opened the door and went inside; he followed her. 'What does he want?' she asked.

'He asked me to go and have a word with him as soon as you got back. It shouldn't take long.'

'You have to go out now?'

'I'm afraid so . . . But it's really good news. He said that the threat of anything happening is now considered to be very much less than when he saw us.'

'I wonder if that's true?'

'Judging by the way he spoke it is.'

'Then why's he in such a hurry that he must see you tonight?'

'He needs some more information about Radlington.'

'What's to stop him coming here to get it?'

'He did apologize for not doing so, but said he's so much work in hand he just can't get away from the office.'

'It surely can't really make any difference if you don't go until tomorrow?'

'He did call it urgent. Of course, I reckon he's the kind of man for whom everything's urgent . . . But anyway, I did say I'd go. The sooner I'm away, the sooner I'll be back.' He opened the front door.

'At least wait long enough to tell me how Bob was while I was away?'

'He went to bed after a bolshie refusal to eat any supper because I would be cooking it and not you. I tried hard to make him see sense, then packed him off without anything. In his dreams, he's no doubt cursing me on all wavelengths.'

She sighed. 'He's not becoming any easier, is he?'

'Time's supposed to solve everything. But what time-scale are we having to operate on?'

'You sound really pessimistic.'

He tried to speak more lightly, to hide from her the fact that the cause for his worry was not Bob's behaviour. 'Only irked that all my logical arguments were scorned and order was only maintained by the threat of a hairbrush on a bare bottom.'

She kissed him on the cheek. 'Thank you for being so patient.'

'For such a reward, I'm prepared to understudy Job. Don't forget to lock and bolt the door as soon as I'm away.'

'Take your stick with you.'

'There's no need . . .'

'Take it, Steve, just in case. It would be too awful if something happened to you because you didn't have it.'

'Nothing can happen to me tonight,' he replied, as he picked it up.

One of the watchers switched the transceiver to send. 'Jim, male target is driving away.'

'It's getting more like Hyde Park Corner every moment. Where's he off to, for God's sake? Didn't he listen to the Guv telling him to keep his feet in front of the fireplace?'

'You know how they think—it can't ever happen to me.'

'How lucky to be innocent . . . Target passing now and no sign of a tail . . . Target out of sight and still on his ownsome. So wherever he's off to, he won't be interrupted.'

CHAPTER 21

Collins drove into the forecourt of the main motel building, then along the drive which gave access to the cabins. He stopped in front of No. 7, behind another car.

He stepped out of the Escort, locked it, crossed to the front door of the cabin and knocked. The door was opened and he entered, to face Moira. He had remembered how attractive she was but not how immediately she aroused a man's hopes and expectations.

'Steve,' she said softly.

'Hullo, Moira.' Her eyes were bright; sparkling would have been a better description. They'd looked like that when they were making love . . .

'It's wonderful seeing you again.'

'It's good to see you.'

Their dialogue was banal, but below the spoken words were unspoken ones which were the antithesis of banal. He recalled one of their more exotic moments of love . . .

'Would you like a drink?'

'Yes, please.'

'Is Glenmorangie still your favourite?'

'When I can afford it, which is every other Christmas.'

She went over to the small and somewhat battered chest of drawers opposite the two beds, opened the top drawer and brought out a bottle. 'And after the meal it was always armagnac in preference to cognac.' She smiled. 'Relax. I'm not building up to an emotional scene. I promised you—no recriminations, just one question and one answer. Sit down while I pour the drinks.'

He sat in the only armchair, which creaked as it took his weight.

'D'you still like it neat?'

'That's right.'

He watched her pour out two strong whiskies and her movements had the same easy, powerful grace as those of a leopard. Her figure was as slim as before. She'd always complained that her breasts were too small to be interesting, but she'd been so wrong . . .

'Do you still dislike it when I want to know what you're thinking?' she asked as she walked towards him.

'It's not a case of dislike, but a reluctance to admit to their vacuity.'

'Still hiding!' She handed him one glass, went over to the nearer bed and sat. She was wearing a full skirt and once seated she smoothed it down with a slow movement which caught his attention before he forced himself to look away.

'What are we going to drink to?'

'Whatever you like.'

'What do you want most in life?'

'Happiness.'

'You're not happy?'

'I'm very happy. I should have said, the continuation of happiness.'

'You like being married?'

'Yes.'

'She's a very lucky woman. I suppose she's much more beautiful than me?'

'Comparisons are not only odious, they are mostly incorrect and meaningless.'

'One thing about you I had forgotten was how smooth your tongue could be.' Her tone gave her words a double meaning. She waited, then said: 'Are you scared of me, Steve?'

'What makes you ask that?'

'You're being so very careful and reserved. What is it?

Worrying because you're a married man in a bedroom with another woman?'

'A sitting-room.'

'It's strange to hear you say that. You never used to hide behind a change of name . . . Don't you remember you once told me that there are only two meaningful distinctions of class in the world, not the rich and the poor, the educated and the uneducated, or the religious and the irreligious, but the conventional and the unconventional. When we were rather unconventional, you used to say we were truly living.' She stared into her memories. 'Yet now it has to be a sitting-room and not a bedroom!'

'It's known as the middle-age syndrome.'

'But I think that in your case it's just a pose.'

'You're wrong.'

'People don't change that much. Deep down, I'll bet you're still unconventional; that you still believe free will means exercising free judgements.'

'Maybe I've grown up enough to learn that one can only afford free judgements when one's very young.'

'We're back to middle age! But you're still a long way from that.' She studied him intently. 'I'm quite sure that in reality you haven't changed a scrap, but you're determined to appear as if you have.'

'How far does one have to pursue appearance before it becomes reality?'

'Tell me.'

'I don't know.'

'Talking like this to you is the most wonderful thing I've done for ages and ages . . . And my saying that doesn't mean you've got to start bringing out the frost.'

'I wasn't.'

'You were about to. You're still scared I'm going to become hopelessly emotional.'

'I doubt you've ever done anything hopelessly.'

'Just one thing and you know exactly what that was . . .
Blast! I've very nearly disgraced myself by becoming sentimental. Switch the frost machine to maximum.'

He laughed.

'Laugh more often, Steve. It makes you quite irresistible.
Perhaps it was your smile which flattened all my defences
so quickly . . . I don't suppose you ever bothered to realize
how near to being a virgin I was when we met?'

'I . . .'

'The question terrifies the man! All right, we'll change
the subject. So what do we talk about? Sealing-wax and
cabbages and kings? What's a suitable quotation for here
and now? "''Tis better to have loved and lost than never to
have loved at all''? How true is that? Is it better never to
have known something wonderful because then you don't
miss it when you haven't got it any longer? I'd have said a
very loud yes at the beginning. But now I think the quote's
probably right. Our time together was truly wonderful.
Now, I can look back on it without becoming all mixed-
up with contrary emotions so that I refuse to admit the
truth . . . You thought it was wonderful too, didn't you?'

'Yes.'

'Can't you be a little more enthusiastic than that?'

'It was great.'

'I suppose that, coming from you, that's wild enthusiasm
indeed!'

He cleared his throat. 'Are you sure that no one else from
Radlington knows I'm living down here?'

'Positive. And because I've learned to look at the past
without bitterness, no one ever will.' She finished her drink,
stood, crossed to his chair. 'Give me your glass.'

As he handed it to her, he smelled her scent and identified
it as the one she had always used. He'd bought her a bottle
one June day. She'd kissed him with a wild passion, stripped,
and demanded he put a dab here, a dab there . . .

'You've disappeared again. Could you be remembering the time you gave me a bottle of scent and we had such fun?'

'Did I give you some?'

'You really can't remember? Then I wonder how much else you've forgotten? How many memories am I treasuring which are just blanks in your mind? Or are you deliberately creating those blanks?'

'It's a whole world ago . . . Look, I'm sorry, but I'll have to leave now.'

'Not before you've had that other drink. And looked me in the face and answered my question.' She walked over to the chest of drawers and refilled the glasses, returned and handed him one. 'I wonder if you ever began to understand just how much I loved you?'

'Of course I did.'

'Was it the same for you?'

'Yes.'

'You didn't say all those things just to get a good screw?'

'No.' She'd always used crude language when they'd made love; she'd claimed that it heightened the pleasure to breach every last barrier of taste.

'And you're not saying that now to make me believe what I want to believe?'

'It's the truth.'

'If you really did love me that much, I could never do anything to harm you.'

A threat implied or a remark made without any deeper import? He didn't know, couldn't judge. Yet if it was a threat and he didn't ease it aside, she could illogically turn violently against him, reverse her previous actions and tell the others where he lived. He had no option but to convince her; the lives of Judith, Bob, and himself, could well depend on that. 'I loved you so much that ever since I haven't dared remember because it would hurt too much.'

'Oh God, Steve, I've waited and waited to hear you say

that! Even when I was stupid enough to think I hated you, I desperately longed to hear it.' She put her glass down on the rickety table by the side of the chair. 'Show me. Show me you're telling the truth.' She took hold of his head and drew it against her body.

He had to free himself if he were not to betray Judith. But reject Moira now and fury would drive her into betraying him . . . She took his right hand and ran it under her skirt. As his fingers caressed her warmth, he ceased to be able to judge, to decide, or even to acknowledge that there was an option.

CHAPTER 22

Judith looked at the carriage clock to the right of the fireplace and frowned. It was nearly two hours since Steve had gone out and yet he'd given no indication that he might be this long. Could something . . . She stopped her thoughts racing on, knowing full well that where her family was concerned, her emotions knew no boundaries. Steve, she told herself firmly, was with the Detective Chief Superintendent and so nothing whatsoever could happen to him.

She yawned, used the remote control to switch off the television, stood. The committee meeting had been a tiring one—how could nine people, all of whom had the same aims, find so much to argue about so pointlessly?

She checked the two outside doors and the ground-floor windows, made her way upstairs to their bedroom. She turned down the bedspread, brought her nightdress out from its case, went through to the bathroom. She was returning along the corridor, wondering how she'd manage to keep awake until Steve returned when she would have to let him in, when the door of Bob's bedroom opened and he stepped out, blinking in the light. 'What in the wide world are you doing out of bed at this time of night?' she asked.

'I'm hungry.' He came forward to be picked up and, after bracing herself to meet his weight, she lifted and cuddled him.

'I'm hungry.'

'Steve tried to give you supper . . .'

'No, he didn't,' he said quickly. 'He wouldn't give me anything.'

'Bob, you know that that's not correct. He wanted to get you your meal, but you wouldn't let him cook it for you.'

'He said I couldn't have anything and if I didn't go straight to bed he'd hit me with a hairbrush.'

She sighed. Perhaps it was being cowardly, but she couldn't face arguing about it at this time of night. 'Are you really hungry?'

'I'm starving.'

'Then we'd better go downstairs and try to find you something.'

'I want beefburgers.'

'I want is made to want. Please may I have.'

'But I'm starving.'

'Until you have collapsed, there's time for manners . . . Get down, put on some slippers and a dressing-gown, and come downstairs. Isn't it a bit late for beefburgers? Why not settle for a jam and peanut sandwich?'

'Beefburgers,' he said, as he dropped to the carpeted floor.

'Then two only.'

In the kitchen, she opened the small chest deepfreeze and brought out two beefburgers, put them in the microwave oven, set the controls, and switched on. She was cutting a second slice of wholemeal bread when he entered the kitchen. After some difficulty, he perched himself on the four-legged stool. 'It's true, he wouldn't let me have anything to eat,' he said fiercely.

'I'm sure it wasn't like that. Perhaps you just didn't understand each other. We'll ask him when he comes back.'

'Perhaps he won't come back.'

Her anger was immediate. 'How dare you say that!'

He was delighted to have caused so sharp a reaction. 'Maybe he's staying with the lady and won't ever come back.'

The pinger on the oven sounded, but she ignored it. 'What lady?'

'The one who phoned him.'

'That was a policeman.'

'It was a lady.'

'How do you know?'

'I answered the phone.'

'Then you spoke to the secretary of a policeman.'

'What's a secretary?'

'A lady who works for someone.'

'He didn't know who she was to begin with. He kept asking her how she'd found him.'

'How do you know that?'

'I was listening at the door after he shut it so I couldn't hear.'

She tried to control her voice. 'You're making all this up, aren't you?'

'No, I'm not. He did shut the door to stop me hearing. And it was a lady. And her name was . . . Something like Mary.'

'Mary Who?'

'I don't know and it wasn't 'xactly Mary.'

'Then what was it like?'

'I can't remember.'

'You've got to try.'

'I'm hungry.'

'I'll get you your meal as soon as you've remembered.'

'But I can't,' he said, aggrieved.

'Was it Moira?'

'That's right. And now can I have my beefburgers; the oven's finished.'

She stared at him for several seconds and her expression began to frighten him. Then she whirled round, went into the hall, checked the telephone number King had given them and dialled it.

CHAPTER 23

Sex, King thought, was responsible for half the troubles of the world; and the other half were caused by lack of it. Collins had been explicitly warned, yet still he'd rushed off after his tart, never once stopping to think that she was the most likely of baits. If he hadn't been responsible for setting the trap, he'd bloody well have left Collins to discover that there could be even more fatal consequences to illicit sex than AIDS.

He dialled the central police station and spoke to his duty liaison officer. 'Our target's taken off after a woman. Ask for an all car search for his red Escort. When it's traced, he's to be located and assistance given.'

'Roger.'

King replaced the receiver. Would they find Collins? If they found him, would it be in time? His own career was riding on the answers.

They passed a signpost. 'Two miles,' said the man in the front passenger seat.

Prescott tried not to visualize what might be happening in the motel room at that moment. His love for Moira caused him as much pain as pleasure; although she had never said so, he judged that his attraction for her lay in the contradiction of his fulgent brain locked inside an ugly body and one day she might search for other forms of perverse charm . . .

'Can't you hurry it up?' demanded one of the two in the back.

They were becoming more scared with every minute, he thought. They were learning that it was easy to threaten death, very difficult to deliver. He braked to a stop at crossroads, even though the absence of other lights showed there was no traffic. He was conscious of the fact that he was driving with exaggerated care because he was almost as reluctant as they, even though nothing could taste sweeter than revenge; revenge for his betrayal, revenge for Moira's betrayal.

They had covered another half-mile when one of them in the back said: 'There's a car coming up fast.'

He looked in the rear-view mirror. The twin lights closed very quickly, then the other car drew out and passed them and they saw that it was a white patrol car.

'It's the police! They've . . .'

He interrupted the man with a violent, 'Shut up!' They were so scared now that it would need little to strip from them the last vestiges of resolve. 'It's nothing to do with us.'

'Something's got to be up with them going at that speed.'

'Someone's just returned home and found he's been burgled.'

The road bore round to the right to join the main coast/ Oakley Cross road. As they passed a garage, closed but with forecourt illuminated, they saw the line of poplars, outlined by the lights behind them, which marked the motel. Over the phone, Moira had said that she was in cabin seven and those on either side were empty. The door would be unlocked, so all they had to do was rush in and smash the life out of the traitor. The others were nervous, but experience proved that when face to face with their victim, fears would turn into a frenzy . . .

'The police car's stopping at the motel,' said the front passenger suddenly.

They could now see past the poplars. The patrol car had passed the turn-in to the motel forecourt, but was stopped, brake lights on. As they watched, the brake lights went off, the white reversing lights came on briefly, the car turned into the forecourt.

'For Christ's sake, they know we're after him,' one of them shouted.

'Get out of it,' shouted another.

They were now in such a cowardly state, Prescott thought bitterly, they wouldn't even try to rescue Moira. On his own, he would be helpless. Sick with despair, he accelerated and they passed the motel.

The sharp knock on the cabin door startled Collins. Moira was no less surprised because Prescott knew that the door would be unlocked.

There was another and louder knock. 'It's the police.'

Her first thought was to run. But she was naked, the only door was the one at the front and that was where her car was.

'Are you in there, Mr Collins?'

She stared at him, hatred momentarily overcoming her panicky fear; but his expression suggested that he'd no idea how the police knew where he was. He had not helped to lay the trap in which she now found herself caught. 'Answer them,' she whispered.

'But . . .'

She had managed to identify her only way of escape. 'If they find me, the others will know where you're living.'

He couldn't be certain whether that was a threat or a statement of fact that if they knew for certain in which area he lived, they'd concentrate on that area and eventually find him. 'What do you want?' he called out.

'Are you Mr Collins; Mr Steven Collins?'

'Yes.'

'Then we'd like a word with you.'

'I . . . I'm busy.'

There was a sound which could have been a laugh suddenly cut short. 'We won't keep you for long.'

She jumped out of bed and grabbed her clothes. 'Admit you've had a woman here, but say she left earlier.' She crossed to the cupboard, stepped inside, pulled the door shut.

'Come on, Mr Collins, hurry it up; we're beginning to take root out here.'

He dressed, ran his hand over his hair to try to smooth it down. He crossed to the door, went to unlock it and found it unlocked. Two policemen in uniform, wearing crash helmets, entered before he could make any move to prevent them.

'You live in Brecks Cottage?' asked the elder PC.

'Yes.'

'My mate saw your car. Have you got any sort of trouble?'

'No, none.'

The bottle of Glenmorangie and two glasses were on the chest of drawers. The younger PC said: 'Been entertaining, have you?'

'What business is it of yours?'

The elder PC spoke in a conciliatory tone. 'Frankly, Mr Collins, we can't rightly answer that. Our orders were to look out for your car and if we saw it to find out if you were safe.'

'Then you can now see that I am.'

The younger PC walked over to the bathroom door and checked inside. He turned and stared at the bed nearer to him; the state of the bedclothes left little room for doubt. 'You're on your own now, then?'

Collins ignored the question and spoke to the elder man. 'I'm leaving.'

'It'll be best if you wait until we've been on the blower to HQ and had a word with them.'

'Am I under arrest?'

'There's no question of that, Mr Collins.'

'There's no law against a bit of slap and tickle,' said the younger PC. He grinned woolfishly.

'Belt up,' said his companion angrily.

'I'm leaving and returning home,' said Collins.

The elder PC shrugged his shoulders. 'If you won't stop until we've had a word . . .'

'I won't.'

'Then that's that.'

'So long as you've settled the bill,' said the younger PC.

Collins walked to the outside door.

'You're forgetting the whisky.'

'Drop it in the wastepaper-basket.'

Not bloody likely, thought the younger PC.

Collins left the cabin. He unlocked the door of the Escort, climbed in behind the wheel, started the engine, drew out past Moira's car and continued on to the turning circle beyond the last cabin, drove back. The two PCs now standing outside the cabin and framed by the light coming through the opened doorway, watched him pass.

It was a warm night, but not warm enough to account for the sweat that was prickling his body. Would they leave immediately, thereby allowing Moira to escape unseen? Or would they find her? Had her words been a threat? . . . And how in the name of God could he have so readily betrayed his marriage?

King, red-eyed, his chin stubbled, his tie loosened and his collar button undone, said: 'Why the bloody hell did you let him go?'

The elder PC, his gaze fixed on the far wall, answered.

'There was no charge to hold him on, sir; leastwise, none that we knew of. All he'd done as far as we could see was shack up with a tart for a quickie.'

King went round the desk and slumped down in the chair. 'Any idea who the woman was?'

'He didn't give us the chance to question him.'

'Who booked in?'

The elder PC looked at the younger, who brought out a notebook from his tunic pocket. 'Miss A. P. Stone from seven, Armsdale Road, West Drayton, sir.'

The elder PC said: 'I've checked and there's no Armsdale Road in West Drayton.'

'Good thinking . . . What chance would anyone inside have had of getting away after you arrived?'

'None. There's only the outside door.'

'Windows?'

'The two windows face the front, where we were.'

'But he'd definitely had a woman there?'

The younger PC said: 'There was an opened bottle of whisky and two glasses; one of the beds looked as if they'd been trying out the *Kama Sutra* for size; he'd obviously just pulled his clothes on.'

If she had already left, then obviously it had been only a quickie. Yet if the woman had been Moira, she surely wouldn't have left before the would-be murderers arrived? 'Did you search the cabin?'

'There wasn't anywhere to search, sir. Just the main room and the bathroom and there wasn't anyone in the bathroom.'

'What about cupboards; under the beds; behind curtains?'

'Can't say we checked; didn't seem no call to do that.'

'The woman could have been hiding, then?'

'I suppose so.'

'There was no one behind the curtains,' said the younger

PC, 'seeing as they didn't reach down to the floor and I'd say the beds was too low for anything much bigger than a mouse to get under 'em.'

'Which leaves the cupboards.'

'There's only one. I suppose that was about big enough,' said the elder PC.

'Then get back and see if there's anything in the cupboard which'll suggest there's been a woman hiding in it.'

Judith was waiting in the hall and when Collins came into view she unlocked and unbolted the front door. As he stepped inside, she said: 'All I want to know is, why?'

'I had to go,' he replied miserably.

'Presumably just as you had to lie and say you were meeting Mr King?'

'You must understand . . .'

'I wish to God I could. But I look at things in a completely different light from you. I'm so old-fashioned I believe marriage means what one promises in church; to love, to honour, and to forsake all others. I suppose you've just never managed to understand that that's the kind of person I am.'

'Of course I have.'

'Then you must be a fool,' she said contemptuously. 'Satisfy my prurient curiosity about the why. What is she offering that I don't?'

'It's not like that . . .'

'Then you're not accusing me of failing to accommodate you in bed as often as, and in the style, you want? I'm surprised. That's apparently what most husbands complain about. Wives with too many headaches and none of the imaginative enthusiasm they'd once shown in the backs of cars . . .'

'Please, stop it.'

'Because you can't bring yourself to admit the truth?'

'Because it's not like that.'

'Isn't it? Be honest for once, if you can remember

how. Have you been having sex with Moira tonight?'

He was silent for a long while, then he said, his voice expressing desperation: 'I had to.'

'Lack of will-power? Or did she threaten you with nameless tortures if you didn't perform?'

'It was because of you.'

'Oh my God,' she murmured. 'Do you have to mock me as well as spit in my bed? Do you hate me that much?'

He stepped forward, she retreated.

'Moira's mentally unbalanced . . .'

'But sexually fully in control.'

'If I'd upset her, she'd have told the others where I'm living.'

'But since you serviced her with professional competence, she won't?'

'I had to keep her friendly.'

'Some obligations obviously come more easily than others.'

'I didn't go there intending to . . .'

'Why the reluctance to put the deed into words? Can you hide the truth from yourself all the time it's unspoken?'

'She seduced me.'

'What does women's lib mean if not equal opportunities in everything? I trust you at least put up an image-enhancing resistance? Did you beg her not to dishonour you? Did you plead with her just to remain good friends? Did you . . .' She stopped as she finally began to cry. He tried to put his arms round her. 'Don't touch me,' she shouted wildly.

'I swear I wouldn't have done it except . . .'

'I'm leaving in the morning.'

'You can't . . .'

'You still don't understand what you've done? Or you've such contempt for me and my old-fashioned standards that you think some fast talking and time will make me forgive . . . I'd leave now, but it's too late at night.'

'Why won't you at least try to understand?'

She crossed to the stairs. 'Your things are in the spare bedroom.' The tears rolled down her cheeks.

CHAPTER 24

When the two PCs returned to King's office, he was half-asleep, sprawled uncomfortably in the chair. He jerked himself upright.

'Nothing concrete in the cupboard, sir,' said the elder PC, 'but Alf reckons he smelled scent.'

King looked at the younger PC.

'I'm sure of it. Like a Baghdad brothel.'

'You're an expert on the subject?'

'No, sir.' The younger PC smiled briefly.

King turned to the elder PC. 'You didn't smell it?'

'No, but that doesn't mean anything. I've never had a good nose and it's becoming worse as I get older.'

Strong scent, thought King, could linger for quite a time in an enclosed space. But from the previous night? Assume a woman had been hiding in the cupboard. Despite the evidence, there could be no absolute certainty that she had been Moira. She might have been a prostitute whom Collins had bundled into the cupboard to hide her from the police and hence, hopefully, from his wife. But if she had been Moira, then only one set of facts seemed to fit the circumstances and they were that she had been acting as bait and the murderers had been on their way, but the police had identified the red Escort in time to forestall them.

'One more thing, sir. There was another car, a Metro, parked near the cabin when we went there the first time and that had gone when we returned.'

In the normal course of events—forgetting prostitutes—

172 A CONFLICT OF INTERESTS

it would be unusual for a guest to leave in the middle of the night. 'I don't suppose you took the number?'

'Afraid not, seeing there didn't seem to be any cause. But it came from Shropshire.'

'How d'you know that?'

'The county letters were UX. I'm from Shropshire, so I always notice.'

It wasn't proof in the legal sense, but it was proof enough for King. Members of a hard cell had set out from Radlington to gain their revenge, but because Collins had been such a bloody fool as to totally ignore the warnings he'd been given, he'd not only just escaped being murdered, the would-be murderers had been warned and had escaped the trap. King slammed his fist down on the desk, making the two PCs start. Now the police were no nearer being able to identify the man or men in charge and so prevent their carrying out the murder of a royal than they had been at the beginning.

Collins drove slowly up to the T-junction and turned right. He felt mentally battered. Excuses, explanations, appeals, had all been rejected. Judith had insisted on going to stay with Susan Moore, a friend who lived on the far side of Oakley Cross and he had driven her there. Her last words had been to say that there was no point in his trying to get in touch with her. Bob had looked really happy . . .

A Rover was parked in front of the garage and he cursed because he needed to be on his own; he cursed even harder when he recognized King. He climbed out of his car, slammed the door shut. 'I can't talk now.'

'I suggest we go inside.'

'Didn't you listen . . .' He stopped. What the hell was the use? King wasn't going to disappear just because it was obvious he was unwelcome.

They walked round to the front door and went inside. In

the sitting-room King stood in front of the fireplace as if he were the man of the house. 'You had a woman at the motel last night.'

'Did I?'

'Despite everything I'd said, when the woman telephoned you went along to the motel without telling me.'

'I wasn't aware that I needed to account to you for my every action.'

'I told you that your life was in danger because word about your present whereabouts had got through to ALFA.'

'You were wrong. Word had reached only two people, one of whom is dead. The other will never pass on the information.' Collins saw King's expression. 'She learned my new name and address from a man who was trying to sell the information. He was killed in an accident before the price was agreed. Now, she's the only person who knows.'

'You really believe all that?'

'Yes.'

'Why?'

'She told me.'

'In order to sucker you. They discovered your name and address and it became her job to lure you to that motel where they intended to murder you. The only reason you're still alive is because you and your stepson had had some sort of disagreement, he heard you have a telephone conversation in the course of which you mentioned the name of Moira, and with a childish instinct of knowing how to hurt, without at all understanding why it should, he mentioned the fact of the call to your wife. She immediately realized the significance and telephoned me. I had a general search and find call put out on your car. If the two PCs had sighted it even a quarter of an hour later, it's my guess it would have been too late for you.'

'You're twisting the facts round to try and make me believe that she was a party to my intended murder because you hope that then I'll become so frightened I'll identify her to you.'

'If you believe that, you're showing very little intelligence.'

'Because I'm not stupid enough to be taken in by you? You don't care what hurt you cause, do you, just so long as you get to where you want? But for you, my wife would not have learned . . . Things would be different.'

'Quite. Your head would be a pulpy mess.'

'Moira was not trying to trap me, she was helping me.'

'Impossible.'

'Prove it.'

His only way of doing that would be to admit that the hard cell in Radlington had learned Sanderson's new name and address because he had deliberately leaked that information to them.

'You can't!'

'In strict terms, perhaps not. But I am quite certain that I am right. I can assure you that you were lured into what was intended to be a one-way trap.'

'It's not an assurance I'll accept.'

'Mr Collins—'

'Look, I've had a hell of a twenty-four hours, thanks to you and your lot. The kindest thing that you can do right now is leave.'

King, observing an unusual degree of self-control, continued to speak quietly and earnestly. 'It's essential that you confirm that the woman you saw in the motel was the same Moira you knew when you lived near Radlington.'

'You've made it clear that you're certain she was.'

'But you must confirm that she was and then identify her. I cannot explain anything more, but I swear on everything that I value that I must know who she is if I'm to prevent a crime being committed which could have very far-reaching, even devastating effects.'

'In what way?'

'I cannot divulge any more.'

'I'm not surprised, since the facts exist only in your mind. You'll try every way there is to trick me into giving you her name. You're not content with what you've done to my life, you want to wreck hers as well. I suppose you're short on promotion and reckon that if you think up a crime and can then be seen to be preventing it, you'll get some brownie points?'

'You're teaching me something, Mr Collins. Education doesn't stop a person being totally ignorant.'

'And you're teaching me something, Mr King. Rank and position sometimes make a man think he stands a hell of a sight taller than he really does.'

'There's little point in continuing.'

'There's none.'

King walked to the door of the sitting-room, his anger and sense of frustration obvious.

The telephone rang on Thursday evening, minutes after Collins had returned home from work. He ignored it and put the kettle on the stove, assuming that the caller was another of their 'friends' ringing up to discover whether the rumours were true. The phone went on ringing. He put an individual china filter unit on top of a mug, searched the store cupboard for a new packet of filter papers and found there weren't any. No decent coffee . . .

The phone was still ringing. Swearing—at the lack of filter papers as much as at the persistence of the caller—he went out into the hall and picked up the receiver.

'Steve.'

The caller was Judith. He knew a sense of shock. He'd convinced himself that their separation was really her fault —her prejudices and unwillingness to accept that a man could faith unfaithfully keep—but he had only to hear her voice to know that it didn't matter a damn whose fault it was so long as they came together again.

'Steve, are you there?'

'Yes,' he answered hoarsely.

'I'm frightened for Bob. I don't know what to do.'

'What's happened? Is he ill?'

'I was late getting to the school to pick him up and he had to wait and a man came up and tried to persuade him to go off to the fair on the common.'

Only that morning there had been a report in the newspaper of a boy of five who had disappeared after being seen with a man no one could identify . . .

'Steve, you've got to help me. I don't know what to do. I'm so frightened, I feel sick.'

'I'll be with you as soon as I can.'

He left the house and hurried round to the garage. On the drive around Oakley Cross, his thoughts raced. As that morning's paper had witnessed, child abduction was an all too common, tragic occurrence. So this might have been one such attempt. But was it only a coincidence that it had happened when it had? Had the man been a pervert with no aim in view other than the gratification of his sexual desires? Or had he been planning a kidnap and subsequent murder because the attempt on the stepfather had failed?

The Moores' house was a rectory which dated from the time when the country parson had often been a man of some material as well as spiritual consequence. It lay back from the road, from which it was separated by a stream and a field. Its one-acre garden was a mass of colour, a Range-Rover was parked before the front door, and a pair of chestnut mares in a paddock with white-painted post-and-rail fencing completed the picture of the wealthy countryfied townsman.

Susan Moore let him into the house and he was unsurprised to see that she was as perfectly groomed as if about to attend a garden party.

'Judith's in the pink room,' she said in her affected voice.

'I'll go through.'

'She's very upset.'

'Yes, of course.'

'Try and be kind to her.'

He wondered if she thought he'd come determined to be cruel?

'I must go. I have to rush off and do some shopping, so I may not see you again.'

She clearly didn't expect him to stay for long. He went down a corridor to the pink room which, for all its elegance, always reminded him of an overgrown boudoir.

Judith and Bob were seated at a games table, playing snakes and ladders. Judith said: 'Steve. Thank God you're here!'

He was shocked to see the signs of strain in her face.

She turned to Bob. 'Go and find Nanny and ask her to take you for a walk.'

'I don't want to go for a walk.'

'Do as you're told,' she said fiercely.

He was so astonished by her sudden anger that without any further argument—but with a look of sharp dislike at Collins—he left.

'Tell me what happened?' said Collins. He sat.

'I'm so scared . . . I went to collect Bob this afternoon in the car that Susan's lent me and it refused to start. The gardener tried to help, but couldn't, so since she was in the Bentley, I borrowed the Range-Rover. I was ten minutes late by the time I reached the school.

'The duty teacher's meant to stay in the playground until all the children have been collected, but something happened, or he was lazy, and he was in the building, leaving Bob in the playground on his own. Bob promises me he didn't go out into the street, but knowing him . . . A man talked to him, gave him a toffee, and asked him if he'd like to go to the fair. They'd actually started off . . .'

As she remained silent, he said: 'After all we've said to him, all the warnings we've given!'

'I can't understand it either. And yet in a way I suppose that maybe I can. He says the man was so friendly and he adores fairs . . . When I drove up, Bob said I was his mother. The man hurried off.'

'Thank God you arrived in time.'

'I promise I couldn't help being late,' she said despairingly.

'I'm not blaming you, not for one second.'

'The teacher should never have left the playground. He tried to explain why he had, but I was so terrified, I wouldn't listen and kept shouting at him like a fishwife.'

'That's what he needed, and a damned sight more. How the hell could the school employ a man who doesn't realize that whatever emergency arises elsewhere, he stays with the kids until they're fetched?'

'If Bob had disappeared because I was a little late, I . . . Oh Christ, I'd have gone crazy!'

He stood, crossed to her and put a hand on her shoulder. She reached up and gripped it.

'Steve, I keep thinking of all the ghastly things I've read about. Children being sexually assaulted and murdered . . .'

She was trembling. 'It didn't happen,' he said. 'Stop thinking about how nearly it did, remember only that it didn't. Have you told the police?'

'I was in such a state when I got back here that Susan had to call them for me. Two detectives came and asked questions. They wanted a description of the man. I just couldn't give them one that meant anything because I was concentrating on Bob and never really looked at the man until he was hurrying away and then all I could see was the back of his head.'

'What did the police say?'

'They'd make inquiries and check up on all known perverts. If I'd been even one minute later, perhaps . . .'

'Love, would it help to come home? I can't explain it as clearly as I'd like, but I'm sure that if the world around you is the normal one you know so well, life can become normal that much quicker.'

The way she gripped his hand even tighter was answer enough.

It was the evening; they'd each had two strong drinks and Judith was beginning to enjoy a degree of mental calmness.

'There's something I must do,' he said, speaking reluctantly.

'What?'

'Ring King and tell him what's happened.'

'Why him when the local police . . . You mean, you think it may not have been a ghastly pervert trying to get hold of a boy . . .?'

CHAPTER 25

King arrived at Brecks Cottage at 4.30 in the afternoon. Collins, who had not gone to the office, met him at the garden gate. 'Have you found out anything?'

The sunlight slanted across King's face, emphasizing both the strength and the stubbornness. 'A very little. But I'd like to talk about it to both Mrs Collins and yourself— is she here?'

They went into the house. Judith offered King coffee, but he refused it, saying he'd only recently drunk a cup.

'Mrs Collins, since your husband rang me last night, I've been working with the local division. I've spoken to the two detectives whom you saw and heard reports from a couple of others who've been working on the case. But before I tell you what progress has been made, will you answer something. What kind of general, overall, impression did you get of the man?'

She was much calmer than she had been the previous evening, yet she still reached out to hold her husband's hand as they sat on the settee. 'I didn't really look at him. I know I should have done . . .'

'There's absolutely no "should have done" about it. Either consciously or subconsciously, you'd realize your son was in danger and that narrowed your field of interest right down.'

Collins was surprised by the quiet warmth in King's voice which suggested a measure of sympathy, a quality he would not have expected.

'I'm not asking you to try to describe him—I accept that, for the most natural reason in the world, you can't. What I am asking is what kind of impression you gained, because it's usually true that one gains an impression about someone before one appreciates detail. Would you say he was young, middle-aged, or old; well or poorly dressed; athletic or out of condition; confident or nervous?'

She thought for a moment. 'I don't think he was old or even middle-aged. He walked away with an easy stride and certainly wasn't at all plump. He was dressed . . .' She was silent for a moment. 'I seem to see him in sports jacket and grey flannels. But if those weren't exactly what he was wearing, his clothes weren't really casual for this day and age.'

'That's good. Now what about colour and type of hair?'

'I'm sorry, but I've no idea.'

'Approximate height?'

'He wasn't either noticeably short or tall . . . And that's really as far as I can go. It's useless,' she ended bitterly.

'Not so. What you've just said goes to confirm what one of the DCs heard this morning. The owner of a newsagent opposite the school playground saw at the time in question a man hanging around, but unfortunately—if quite under-standably—didn't appreciate there was any cause to be-come suspicious. He described this man as being in his mid-twenties, pleasant, even cheerful, tidily dressed.

'Such a description obviously doesn't help in any positive sense, since it would fit a sizeable proportion of the popu-lation; but in a negative sense, it does tell us something—there was nothing furtive about this man; indeed, "pleasant, even cheerful" suggests the opposite.

'Unfortunately for us, there's no such person as the typical sex pervert; he comes in all shapes, sizes, and ages. But a considerable proportion of perverts do possess a quality—which I can't begin to define—which instinctively raises the hackles of a normal person. Had this man been trying to lure your son away for his perverted sexual gratification, it's more than possible that either or both of you—that is, you and the shop owner—would have recorded a sense of instinctive revulsion and dislike. Please note, I'm saying more than possible, not certainly.'

'Then I could be right,' said Collins, 'and this wasn't a man on the prowl, he was attempting to kidnap Bob?'

'As things stand, that seems the more likely.' King spoke to Judith again. 'I'm sorry if what follows causes you pain, but I think it has to be said. The other evening your husband was phoned by a woman whom he'd known many years before. She persuaded him to meet her at the Orchardgreen Motel. Her aim was to hold him there, using the means which came most easily to her, until her companions arrived to murder him.'

'Are you saying that she . . . that she and Steve . . .'

'Your husband, Mrs Collins, was deliberately entrapped. The murder attempt failed only because the police arrived before the would-be murderers. Our reconstruction of events is that when the two constables arrived, she hid in the cupboard in the bedroom.' King looked at Collins, who finally nodded. 'As that attempt had failed, they decided to gain their revenge in another way and since your husband was clearly under close police protection, they settled on a much softer target, your son.'

'They'd have killed him, for no reason?'

'They had reason, however warped and twisted.'

Collins spoke harshly. 'They've failed twice. What happens now?'

'I have to say that I think it likely there'll be a third attempt. These people have to be judged by the standards of fanaticism and history shows that fanatics will pursue a target against all odds and reason.'

'Oh God!' exclaimed Judith. 'Then they may try again to kidnap and kill Bob?'

'Any one of you may become the target.'

'We've got to have police protection,' said Collins.

'I owe it to you, after all that you've been through, to be absolutely frank. We will, of course, give the three of you all the protection we can. But one has to face certain facts. It's virtually impossible to prevent an act of terrorism if the person making it is sufficiently fanatical not to worry about what happens to himself. Time must work against both you and us. It calls for a number of police officers to give twenty-four-hour protection to a person. While they can be maintained in the field for a while, should time pass and nothing happens, inevitably pressure grows to have them reassigned to other duties because even when at full strength, the police never have enough men to carry out all the work they're called upon to do.'

'You're saying we're going to remain at risk and after a

time the police won't protect us and we'll be on our own?'

'That is the situation, put in its bluntest terms.'

'Christ, it's the police's job to protect us!'

'It's our job to protect everyone. When or if that becomes impossible, we have to decide on priorities. I've tried to suggest how we have to go about doing that.'

'Then do something now to stop them.'

'If we were able to identify any one of the persons concerned, we would have a lead that would enable us to identify all of them. Once identified, we could make certain their threat was contained. Unfortunately, we have no such lead.'

In his mind, Collins saw Judith scrumpled up on the ground, her mouth twisted in the rictus of death. 'Moira Durack,' he said.

Judith, in her nightdress, sat on the edge of the bed. She watched her husband pull on his pyjama coat. 'When you tried to tell me what happened at the motel between you and that woman, I called you a liar.'

'Which is hardly surprising.'

'You didn't go there with the idea of bedding her, did you?'

'I went because I judged I didn't dare refuse. When she made a pass, I was certain I still had to humour her because she's so mentally unpredictable. After a while . . .' He stopped.

'After a while, you stopped judging.'

'Yes,' he mumbled.

'You just sacrificed yourself for the sake of the family?'

He thought she was being bitterly sarcastic, but then he realized from her expression that she could find humour as well as heartbreak in the situation. The memory would always hurt; she'd never fully understand how passion had so completely overwhelmed loyalty; but she would accept and forgive. He went across and she welcomed him.

A childhood jingle dropped into King's mind. No more Latin, no more French, no more sitting on the old school bench. He packed a file into his briefcase. No more working in this small, dusty, smelly office; no more restaurants with fine-sounding menus, but tasteless food; no more bitter frustration because a man could talk, but wouldn't . . .

There was a quick knock on the door and Grafton entered. 'You wanted a word?'

'Tell our blokes to pack their bags. I can give three of you a lift back in the car if you're ready inside a quarter of an hour.'

'We're finished?'

'He's given us her name, so now we can start rolling up the whole bunch of murdering maniacs.'

'I'll tell you one thing for certain, Guv. Offer me the George Cross and I'll not take such a risk again! All the time I was chatting up the kid and feeding him toffees, I was expecting to be lynched.'

'It's only the good who die young.'

Grafton left. King picked up the last file on the desk and wedged it into his overfull briefcase. He looked round the room to make certain that he was leaving nothing behind. Nothing, that was, beyond his honour as a policeman, something he'd lost when he'd decided that the only way left in which to make Collins talk was to frighten him into giving Moira's full name.

It was eight months later, after Lees had been arrested and reduced to a blubbering wreck by fear and humiliation, that King learned that his sacrifice had been totally unnecessary since the intended assassination of a royal had never been anything more than a figment of Lees's imagination . . .

THE END